THE SEARCHING GUNS

THE SEARCHING GUNS

Ray Hogan

SAGEBRUSH
Large Print Westerns

First published in Great Britain by ISIS Publishing Ltd.
First published in the United States by Signet Books

Published in Large Print 2010 by ISIS Publishing Ltd.,
7 Centremead, Osney Mead, Oxford OX2 0ES
by arrangement with
Golden West Literary Agency

The moral right of the author has been asserted

British Library Cataloguing in Publication Data
Hogan, Ray, 1908–
    The searching guns.
    1. Western stories.
    2. Large type books.
    I. Title
    813.5'4–dc22

ISBN 978–0–7531–8509–4 (hb)

Printed and bound in Great Britain by
T. J. International Ltd., Padstow, Cornwall

CHAPTER
ONE

It was the buzzards — huge, broad-winged meat eaters circling silently overhead — that Dan Guthry saw first when he opened his eyes.

He stirred weakly. A thousand devils from hell were hammering away inside his skull and a sliver of live fire blazed hotly on the side of his head. Groaning, he endeavored to sit up. Oddly, his left arm seemed lifeless, detached. Looking slowly, carefully, he saw the sleeve of his shirt was matted with blood.

Anger and frustration overrode pain. That bastard of a Rich had shot him twice after dumping him off the saddle! He lay back. Rising, at that moment, was too much of an effort.

Again his glance sought the hot steel sky. The buzzards were still there. His movements had discouraged them not at all. Old hands at the business, they knew their moment would come — the time when they could glide down silently, land, and in that awkward, hopping way of theirs, close in . . . There'd be nothing unskillful in the manner with which they'd use their merciless hooked beaks and powerful talons . . . They'd have him shredded and down to bone in short order.

"I'm not dead yet!" he croaked, lifting his good arm and shaking a fist at the threatening shadows, now beginning to drop lower. Immediately the huge birds soared upward, resumed a higher plane and their patient circling.

He wasn't too far from town, he realized that, but the posse would never find him where he lay. They would be searching to the east — and he was well south of the settlement . . . That damned Sul Rich was a cute one; he'd struck out in one direction, cut back into another.

Guthry, squeezing his eyelids down to slits in order to minimize the painful glare of the sun, stared off to the south. Maybe Rich wasn't as smart as he thought; there was nothing that way — only the Maxwell place a long day's ride off, and beyond it the Espantoso, a waterless sink of blistered land filled with glittering sand, starved cacti, brush and little else. Only those who knew well that vast, heat ravaged world claimed by the Apaches dared venture far into it.

And Sul Rich was a stranger to the country. A wild, uncivilized, animal of a man to whom savagery was a way of life — *and a murderer who escaped from me,* Guthry thought bitterly. *Just when people were beginning to have confidence, decide I could do a lawman's job, this had to happen.*

An oath slipped from his cracked lips, and again he struggled to rise. He must get on his feet, make it back to Lawsonville, mount a horse and start after Rich. The killer had to be caught, brought back — hanged by the neck until dead for what he'd done to the Parsons girl, to her pa — to the judge and the others.

2

He managed to sit up. Instantly his brain began to spin furiously, and suddenly he was sick, heaving from the very bottom of his six foot body. But he doggedly maintained his position, fought off the nausea and allowed it to pass. When it was finally over, he tipped his face to the hovering scavengers, bared his teeth in a mirthless grin.

"Not yet — damn you," he mumbled weakly.

Another spasm of nausea claimed him, but it was over with quickly. He looked around, struggling to see through the haze that clouded his eyes, aware now of a dull throbbing in his arm, harsher pain in his head.

A curious desire to just sit, do nothing, filled him. He had to fight that, he realized. He'd lost a lot of blood and it had turned his legs to jelly, left him with no sand and the inclination to simply stay put, make no effort to reach the settlement.

Only he had to. It was part of the job. It was what that sheriff's star pinned inside the pocket of his dusty, sweat and blood soaked shirt said was expected of him. He was a lawman and it was up to him to keep going. He wasn't supposed to be like other men. He couldn't quit, take the easy way out. He had to pick himself up, regardless, get on the trail of that coldblooded killer who'd made a fool of him.

That galled like a Mexican spur. Sul Rich had fled Lawsonville, riding double with him on the saddle, a pistol jammed so hard in his side that it had drawn blood.

"Line out for them buttes!"

That had been the redheaded outlaw's shouted command as they raced down the street. He'd looked desperately for a chance to knock the killer's weapon aside, spill him from the horse, but it hadn't come.

They'd reached the bluffs east of town unopposed, ducked into the dense brush and scrub trees that clothed the slope below. There Rich had forced him to veer north for a short distance, and then on a rocky shoulder, reverse course and strike south.

It was a clever move originating in a cunning, twisted mind. The posse that surely would get organized and under way within very few minutes after the escape would rush for the buttes, lose all sign in the rocks — and begin a useless search throughout the wrong area.

The killer wouldn't head south for the Espantoso, they'd say. No man in his right mind would seek escape in that burning hell . . . What they'd be forgetting was that Sul Rich didn't know about the Espantoso. One direction was as good as another as far as he was concerned.

Dan sleeved away the sweat glistening on his face. He was getting a bit stronger, it seemed to him. And his vision was clearing. He looked to the sky again. The vultures were still there, refusing to give up on what appeared a sure thing . . . They might even turn out to be of some help . . . Someone in the posse could notice them, get to thinking — wondering.

He lowered his face, blinking hard to relieve the momentary blindness imposed by the sun's direct glare. He swallowed — or tried. Thirst was beginning to get to him. His mouth seemed filled with cotton — dry, hot cotton. *Forget it* . . . . The nearest water was in town five, maybe six miles away. *If you want water get on your feet and start moving* . . .

Why the hell doesn't somebody see those stinking buzzards?

Forget that, too . . . *Man's a fool to hope — depend upon somebody else. Man has to do everything for himself. Nobody looks out for you. Up to you — and you alone* . . . *Make up your mind to that, Mister Sheriff Guthry.*

Sheriff!

Hell, he wouldn't make a pimple on a good lawman's nose! It had happened twice now — once back up in Miles City, now here in Lawsonville . . . Best thing he could do was turn in his star — after losing a prisoner like Sul Rich — go back to riding trail, nursing cows — anything but packing a badge.

Who the hell was he fooling? Nobody . . . The folks in Lawsonville sure wouldn't have any faith in his abilities now . . . And he could forget Cathren Keel, the newcomer who'd moved into town a week or so ago, too. That friendliness she'd shown to him would end; she'd have no use for a loser.

Dan Guthry's wandering, erratic thoughts came to a stupefied halt as his wavering gaze picked up the hoof prints of Rich's horse bearing directly away from the sandy coulee in which he was sitting. He was beginning to remember more; things were coming back to him . . . If only he could shake his head, clear away the haze of cobwebs! But he knew better than to try; such would

5

start him heaving again and there wasn't anything left inside to throw up.

They'd halted in the coulee . . . The horse had been running hard, was wheezing and trembling from the strain of carrying double at a fast gallop. Guthry had felt the gouging in his side lessen, and quickly then was aware of the hard, round pressure of the pistol's muzzle behind his ear.

"Far as you're going, Sheriff!"

The outlaw's voice had a cracked, unnatural pitch to it. Rich was some kind of a wild, savage loony, Dan had decided in that moment. The things he'd done, the way he'd acted, the crazy words he'd uttered — and he wasn't too long a full grown man, either. Nineteen, maybe twenty, he'd never say for sure. Certainly he was no older than that. But age sure as hell had nothing to do with the killing instinct — nothing at all.

"You won't get far," he recalled saying. "Better drop that gun, Sul, turn yourself over to me. The law —"

"Sure," the outlaw had cut in, and the next thing Dan Guthry knew his senses were reeling and he was falling from the saddle.

He'd struck the ground hard, taking the spill on one shoulder. Instinctively he tried to roll away. Another stunning blow to the head had rocked him. Lights had popped before his eyes, and everything around him — the rim of hills, the clumps of rabbitbrush, the balls of snakeweed — all had danced madly through his vision.

Sand had filled his mouth, his nostrils, his eyes as his face was slammed against the hot ground. Pain roared

6

afresh through his flagging senses as Rich had kicked him brutally in the ribs, rolled him to his back.

Barely conscious, he realized the outlaw was going through his pockets, taking the few coins, the fold of currency he was carrying. Then came stillness, a brief period of suspension broken finally by the rank smell of urine, the feel of wet warmness on his legs. From somewhere in the distance words came to him.

"That's what I think of you and your goddam law, Sheriff . . . That — and this —"

Everything was blanked out in the next instant as a terrible force accompanied by a deafening roar slapped hard against his head.

Sul Rich had shot him twice as he lay there, but he'd not known about the second bullet — the one that had ripped into his arm. Afterwards the outlaw had ridden off, evidently believing him dead. The wound above his ear would have given rise to that conviction. He'd bled like a stuck hog. The second shot had simply been for good measure — a final gesture of contempt.

Guthry licked at his parched lips. He felt stronger. No tower of strength, of course, but if he could somehow manage to stand, maybe he could stay that way. That damned spinning inside his head would have to stop, though. Hunkered there in the brush he wouldn't even be seen if someone did happen to notice the buzzards and came to look around . . . Fool to hope for that, but he'd best try getting on his feet, anyway . . . Try . . .

Placing his right hand, palm down, Dan rested his weight upon it, rolled slowly to his knees. Giddiness swept over him in a swirling wave, but he refused to settle back, simply hung there, stubbornly waited for it to pass. The universe motionless once again, he drew himself back until he was sitting on his legs. Then, gathering strength, he forced himself to rise.

For several moments he swayed uncertainly, came near to toppling, but that, too, eventually passed and afterwards, surprisingly, he didn't feel so terribly bad. He grinned bleakly . . . So far, so good — but it was one hell of a long walk to town; and he'd have to hang on to consciousness, not allow himself to fall. He just might not make it back onto his feet a second time.

But he'd make it somehow. He had to — if only to beat those stinking buzzards still hanging around, waiting to sink their beaks into his carcass.

CHAPTER
TWO

"Was three weeks ago . . ."

Dan Guthry mumbled the words as he stumbled on beneath the blazing August sun. Pain was wracking his body. His arm was a lead weight hanging stiff at his side. His brain was a feverish whirl in which consciousness waged a disorderly battle against insensibility — a battle wherein thought was the only weapon . . . *Think . . . Remember . . . Don't let the darkness close in . . .*

It had all started three weeks ago. The Parsons Place — a homestead north of town about ten miles . . . There was a girl. Her name was Henrietta and she was taking a bath in the creek. She was only seventeen years old.

Sul Rich rode up, saw her. Waited in the brush, grabbed her when she came out — raped her and then beat her to death. Her pa heard her screaming but he got there too late . . . Rich gunned him down. Four bullets. The hired hand heard the shots . . .

Guthry was on his knees. He couldn't recall falling, but he was down, hot sand burning the palms of his hands, goatheads piercing the skin, stinging. Muttering, cursing, he struggled back to his feet, fought to get his thoughts lined up once more.

The hired hand — heard the shots. Rode over to see what was going on. Found the girl — then her pa. Saw Rich running off. Was heading into a box canyon west of the place . . . Came riding for me, hell for leather. I went after Rich, caught him. Brought him in. Meek as a lamb but had eyes like a rattler . . . Almost had us a lynching. Would've, too, if it hadn't been for Lawson. And Doc Borden, and Gannon. All stood by me . . .

He had no breath, was sucking wildly for air. A squat cedar stood in his path. He staggered to the tough little shrub, clawed at its branches for support. He looked ahead through haze clouded eyes. Town was there, somewhere. How far? Three miles? Four? Could be a hell of a lot more. He had no idea how much ground he'd covered. A hundred miles, it seemed. Maybe only one.

Mouth gaping, knees trembling, he glanced at the sky. The damned birds were still there, following him, waiting for him to go down — and not rise. They knew how to bide their time; they knew when the moment was right to move in. Sucking deep, he summoned strength, moved on.

What was he thinking about? Oh, Rich — the killings. The trail . . . Judge finally got there. Was the day — let's see — the day before yesterday. Yes, that was it . . . Took a long time getting things ready. Jury, witnesses, all that. Trial started this morning — yes, this morning. Sul Rich was smart. Laughed all the time. Poked fun. Said everybody was lying. Flat claimed he didn't kill the girl or her pa. *Everybody knew he was the one doing the lying. That Rich is some kind of a loony . . . The worst kind . . .*

Jury decided he was guilty real quick. No doubt of it. Had the girl's blood all over his clothes. Face was all scratched from her trying to fight him off. And that hired hand saw him running away. Only verdict a jury could come up with . . .

Was that smoke hanging in the sky? Maybe it was only a cloud — or it could be his eyes were still playing tricks on him. Seemed to be swimming around in his head. Everything was so damned bright — so blinding! . . . Could be smoke, all right. Town wasn't far, if it was.

He caught at a clump of greasewood, steadied himself, rested. The wound in his arm was bleeding again. He'd busted something open when he fell, he guessed. Place on his head seemed all right, just felt stiff and crusted over. Still burned and smarted to beat hell — but that was good. Along with trying to remember every detail of Rich's crimes, it helped keep him conscious and on his feet.

Gathering himself, he staggered on, once again striving to concentrate . . . *Jury found Sul Rich guilty. Judge got ready to pass sentence. Hang from the neck until dead, dead, dead. Judge said it three times. What Rich had coming to him. People in courtroom clapped. Then that damned messenger came in. Henson, said his name was . . .*

Had important letter from the Capitol for the judge. Had to deliver it right then. Judge told him to bring it up, he'd recess court for a couple of minutes. Henson started to do it . . .

Was my fault from then on. Never noticed he still had his gun on. You never let anybody in a courtroom with a weapon except the lawman in charge . . . Was my fault. Never should've let Henson come in without telling him to shuck his iron first . . .

Dan Guthry, weaving precariously, came to a shaky halt. Twisting, face distorted, he glared at the dark, silent observers drifting overhead. "You hear, you black bastards? Was my fault! I let him walk right in there, wearing that gun!"

Gasping, he fell silent in the driving sunlight, a bent, tortured figure fighting to stay on his feet, retain comprehension, and gather strength enough to press on. He stared out over the shimmering flat, stupefied from pain, exhaustion. Where the hell was that town?

Couldn't be far now — but he could be wrong. Maybe he wasn't even going in the right direction; maybe he was stumbling around in circles. He cursed the thought, took a step forward, another — and was again under way.

Sul Rich grabbed that Henson's gun — grabbed it when the damned fool walked by. Jammed it into my belly. Took my pistol, too, then, almost before I knew what had happened. Then he shot the judge — through the heart. Coldblooded as a snake. Took two more shots at the jury. Killed Abe Gilmore. Fred Williams will probably die . . . May have by now.

Then he started backing for the door, holding one gun on me, other on the crowd in the courtroom.

Hostage, he said I was . . . His ticket out of town. We got outside. Only one horse was handy — Henson's. Made me climb aboard and he got on behind me. Kept that gun digging into my guts, other one ready for anybody that got in the way . . .

Rode out of town like that. Nobody tried stopping us. Good thing. That crazy sonofabitch would have killed them sure — right along with me . . .

Guthry paused, half turned, shook his fist at the vultures. "You'd've liked that, damn you! You wouldn't have to hang around — wait. I'd been already laid out for you. Me and a couple others. You could've feasted 'til your gut busted!"

He clawed at his throat. God, but he was thirsty! Man could go a spell without grub, but water was something else. Man had to have water. There'd be plenty in town. Just keep going — and thinking.

All the time we were riding, Rich kept jabbing me with that gun and raving wild like. Told me what a time he had with the Parsons girl. How she fought him . . . And her pa. Mad clean through, he was. Come at him like a she-bear looking out for her cub . . . Took four slugs to stop the old bastard, he said.

We headed south. Not aiming to leave a trail for somebody to follow. Going to fool them good. Reckon he did. Nobody came this way . . . Nobody . . .

Guthry halted, swaying, shook a fist at the hovering birds. "Nobody but you, you stinking, filthy, grave robbing scavengers!"

A frown pulled at his features as he faced the brassy sky. Strangely, the broad winged vultures were drifting away. He glared at them in stupefied silence. Then, again shaking his fist, he shouted: "Keep going! Get the hell away from me! You're not picking my bones — not even if I have to crawl —"

Guthry ceased his shouting abruptly. He'd heard a voice — or had he? Maybe his ears were beginning to trick him now, like his eyes. Jaw sagging, shoulders slumped, head slung forward, he listened. There was only the persistent buzzing of flies attracted by his wounds and the loud, rapid clacking of a cicada, silenced briefly by his approach.

He heard it again. It sounded like a call, coming from close by. Something blurred across his vision. A man on a horse took shape . . . A familiar man — face.

"Sheriff?" a voice said questioningly.

CHAPTER
THREE

The features of the rider swam in and out of focus, became momentarily definite. Guthry's voice was a hopeful croak.

"Gannon?"

"It's me, all right. Mighty glad I found you."

The afternoon quiet split with the sound of two quick gunshots as Gannon summoned the remainder of the posse. Vision still inconstant, Dan watched the rider dismount, hurry toward him.

"Others'll be here in a minute. Then we'll get you to Doc Borden . . . That killer get away?"

Guthry felt the man's arm slip about him, lend him support. He moved his head slightly, mumbled: "Got away. Couldn't stop him. Need a horse — start chasing —"

"Sure, sure. Pretty quick. You hurt bad? Look like you've been to hell and back."

Horses were pounding up. Voices were shouting questions, and suddenly men were all around him, milling about. Dan felt hands guide him to Gannon's mount, boost him onto the saddle. The horse grunted as Gannon swung up behind, and for one flashing interlude of time his mind lapsed and he thought he was with Sul Rich again, only he couldn't feel the pistol barrel gouging into his ribs.

"Take him straight to Doc's," a voice said.

"What I'm aiming to do," Gannon snapped tartly, and moved off.

"Reckon we'd as well head back, too," another voice, barely audible in the haze, reached Dan. "Can't do nothing 'til the sheriff tells us what happened — and it's getting late."

Dan Guthry tried to speak up but thirst locked his voice inside his throat and the best he could raise was a dry rasping noise. Too, he was having trouble thinking straight as pain once more poured through him in a steady stream, occasioned by the motion of Gannon's mount. Each time a hoof came down, met solid earth, a razor edged knife slashed at his head, and a mighty force yanked on his arm. Finally, and mercifully, he became aware of none of it.

Gannon's deep voice, carefully muted, cut through the mist, registered on Guthry's mind.

"Heard all this yelling. Rode over to see what the hell — and there he was. Standing there cussing out the buzzards I reckon had been following him. Was plenty spooky, I'll tell you."

"Showed sense . . . " That was Doc Borden. He had a clipped way of speaking, like he was sore at somebody. "Knew he had to keep his wits, or fall down and die. Was yelling at the buzzards so's he wouldn't pass out."

16

Dan stirred, looked around. He was on a bed in Borden's office. A half dozen men were in the room. He felt only a vague throb of pain, and there was a tightly bound sensation to his arm and head. Bandages, he realized. And Borden had given him something to ease the pain. Laudanum, probably. He must have taken in some water, too. His throat no longer had that burning, cracked feeling.

"He's waking up."

Immediately there was a shuffling sound as the men crowded forward. Dan looked up into a small sea of faces. In the fore were Borden, Gannon and the mayor of the town, Henry Lawson.

Lawson, his features serious, said: "You feeling some better, Sheriff?"

"Some," Guthry admitted. His voice seemed strange to his own ears.

"You won't get much out of him, Henry," Borden said. "Not tonight, anyway. Maybe in the morning —"

"Can't wait for morning," Lawson replied, all business. "That killer's on the loose. Got to decide what's to be done about him."

The physician shrugged, fell back among the others. Lawson moved in close, hunkered beside the bed.

"Sheriff — you hear me? It's the mayor."

Guthry nodded. It was cool, shadowy in the room. Lawson's voice was an intrusion.

"Got to figure what we're going to do about that killer you let — that escaped. You tell us which way he went?"

Again Guthry nodded. "South — the Espantoso."

A long sigh escaped Lawson, one of helplessness. "The Espantoso," he muttered. "Oh, hell."

"Tomorrow," Guthry said, "I'll go get him."

"Not tomorrow, you won't," Borden snapped from the back of the room. "And maybe not the next — or the next."

"Tomorrow," the lawman repeated stubbornly. "Know that country. Nobody else around does."

"He's right," Lawson said, coming to his feet. "Only him and maybe a couple others living close know it good enough to ride in very far."

"And if you did find a couple others you'd play hell talking them into going," someone else commented. "Ain't no time worse'n right now to go sashaying down into that hell hole."

Gannon said: "We can make up another posse, outfit it for a long trip, have it ready to ride when the sheriff's able."

Lawson glanced at Borden. "When'll that be, Doc?"

The medical man pushed forward. "Well, his wounds aren't too serious. Loss of blood mostly. Could be a bit of concussion from that bullet that grazed him — or from those raps he got on the head, too."

"So?"

"You think I'm some kind of a fortune teller? It's hard to answer a question like that, damn it! But he's healthy — got the constitution of a mule. He'll bounce back fast. If you're pinning me down, my guess is it'll take three, four days."

They were discussing him as if he were a prize bull or a good horse, Guthry thought from the depths of the

18

vague, soft edged world through which he seemed to be drifting. Hell, he could fork a saddle right then — or at least in a couple of hours or so. Given a shot or two of good whiskey . . .

"Reckon that's it then," Lawson said heavily. "Nothing we can do but wait. Soon as he's able, it'll be up to him to take a posse in after Rich, drag him back —"

"No posse," Guthry mumbled.

Gannon swore. "You mean you're aiming to go after him alone?"

"One man — no dust. Posse'll raise a cloud he'd see for ten miles."

Lawson rubbed at his chin. "Knows what he's talking about, even if Doc did fill him full of dope. Bunch of riders moving through the Espantoso would stir up a hell of a lot of dust. That killer'd spot them sure."

"So would the Apaches," Tom Pillsbury said from the back of the room.

"Maybe they'll get the job done for us, nab him themselves," another voice said hopefully.

There was a pause. Finally Henry Lawson said: "As soon they wouldn't. That reply I got from the Governor after I sent him a telegram telling him what'd happened, made it plain we'd better catch Rich quick and hang him — or we can expect a company of soldiers to be quartered here in town for a while . . . We sure don't want that."

"Amen," Gannon murmured.

"I'll get him," Guthry mumbled thickly. "Go by myself . . . My job. Was me who let him get away —"

"An accident!" Doc Borden broke in sharply, bending close to the lawman's ear. "You keep blaming yourself. Been mumbling that ever since they brought you in. Get it into your mule head that it was an accident — hear? Nobody faulting you for what happened."

"My prisoner — escaped . . . Should've been more careful. People'll think I —"

Borden swore. "That pride of yours — going to get you killed if you don't watch out. And riding down into the Espantoso alone is a long step in that direction."

"Got to — anyway," Guthry muttered, having difficulty not only with his thoughts but with his words as well. He seemed to be sliding down into a bottomless pit, and fight as he would, he was powerless to halt himself.

"Maybe I can fix that," Henry Lawson said. "Something just come into my mind. Only about half the Espantoso is in this county. Our jurisdiction — the sheriff's — ends there, actually."

"Meaning he wouldn't have any authority once he crossed the line into the next county, that it?" Gannon said.

"Exactly. Oh, sure, I know we've never paid any attention to that, mainly because there's never been any reason to. Same applies to the officials in the other county. They feel like we do about that sink — leave it to the Apaches, and welcome."

"You got a point you're driving at, Henry?" Borden asked testily.

20

"I have. What we need is a U.S. marshal. He could ride with Guthry. The two of them could handle Sul Rich and do it without bringing the Apaches down on their necks."

Borden nodded. "Somebody had better go along with him. He just might play out. No way of knowing what effects he'll get from those raps on the head."

"We'd be calling the Governor's hand, too, sort of. Be letting him know we expect some cooperation from the Territorial Government on the legal part."

"I think you've got something there, Henry," Gannon said, nodding slowly.

"Know dang well I have. Up to the Governor to give us a little help, I'd say. Hell, this Rich wasn't one of our people — not even somebody who lived around close. He's an outsider who was just passing through."

"Whole thing happened by chance. If he hadn't come across the Parsons girl frolicking around in that creek jaybird naked, we wouldn't be standing here now talking about it. There never would've been no killings. You look at it that way, I'd say the responsibility is as much the Territory's as it is ours."

Gannon stared down at Guthry's slack features. "He ain't going to like your ringing somebody else in on his job. He's plenty touchy about things like that."

"He'll just have to like it," Lawson said crisply. "I'm mayor of this town . . . Anyway, he'd be a fool to try it alone, according to Doc. Besides, he'll need the authority to cross the line."

"That's splitting a hair pretty fine," Pillsbury said, wagging his head. "Better get a few more reasons thought up, Henry."

"Not splitting hairs at all! How can we tell Rich will still be in the Espantoso? Could be he'll have made it through by the time Guthry catches up. Might be in Texas or Arizona — even Mexico. The sheriff'll sure need a U.S. marshal with him then."

"Reckon he will, but if I was you I'd tell him about it . . . Now."

"Aim to. Thing I got to look out for is what's best for the town — whether the sheriff likes it or not. We've got to keep remembering he did let a killer escape, no matter how you look at it."

"Now, wait a minute there, Henry —" Borden began but Lawson waved him aside, squatted next to Guthry's bed.

"Sheriff," he said, "listen to me. Might be you'll have to chase Sul Rich clear into the next Territory once you start after him. Means you'll need special authority to make an arrest. I'm sending to Santa Fe for the U.S. marshal to ride with you. Then you can go anywhere. That all right?"

"No posse," Dan Guthry mumbled.

"Be no posse. Just you and a marshal."

The lawman stirred in the pit where he seemed now to be hovering between sleep and wakefulness.

"Marshal — don't need him."

"Yes, you will, Sheriff. You'll be crossing the line."

"Don't want anybody —"

22

Lawson got to his feet. "Nothing I can do but overrule him. You all can see that. I'll get off a telegram to the Governor right away. Time the marshal gets here, Guthry ought to be on his feet, ready to travel."

"He will," Borden said brusquely, "if he can get some rest. You through, Henry?"

Lawson nodded, stepped back as the physician pushed in ahead of him, reached for Guthry's wrist.

"Then get out, all of you. And tell that bunch outside I don't want any of them coming in here. This man's got to get some sleep."

CHAPTER
FOUR

Henry Lawson paused just outside the doorway leading in from Borden's porch, studied the two score or so persons gathered in the street awaiting word of Guthry's condition. Gannon, Pillsbury and the others who had been with him in the room shouldered on by, murmuring as they passed.

When they had crossed the weedy yard and moved through the gateless opening in the sagging picket fence, Lawson moved to the front of the porch, raised both arms to draw attention to himself. After all, he was the mayor; it was his right to make the necessary announcements seeing as how he was what might be considered the official source.

"Friends," he called in a strong voice.

Those who had pressed in upon Gannon and the men with him for information, immediately turned, and the hubbub died. Lawson permitted the hush to run on for a few moments, his eyes roaming over the faces waiting expectantly. Most of them he knew, being residents of the settlement, but there were a scatter of strangers — curious passersby, he supposed, who'd mixed in the crowd, wondering what all the excitement was about.

"Friends," he said again.

"You've done mentioned that," a voice spoke up from the back of the assemblage. "What we want to know is how's the sheriff?"

Henry Lawson frowned, tried to single out the detractor, failed. "He's going to be all right. Had himself a rough time with that killer, but nothing serious happened to him. Be up and around in a couple or three days, Doc Borden tells me."

"Couple of days!" a woman's voice repeated in horror. "With that murderer running loose we could all get killed in our beds!"

Lawson squinted into the lowering sun . . . Hank Lancaster's wife. One of the pillars of the church.

"You'll be safe, Martha," he said. "Sul Rich has skipped the country — headed south."

"South? Into the Espantoso?"

That was Marve Bascomb. Worked in the bank . . . Henry Lawson prided himself on knowing everybody. Since he was the mayor and owned the general store, plus the fact it was his pa who'd founded the town, given it a name, it was a sort of duty. Wasn't such a cinch anymore, however.

The population of Lawsonville was nudging seven hundred, and when you added to that another three hundred souls who lived elsewhere in the county but came in to trade, you had quite a few people. He guessed maybe he couldn't really expect to know everybody.

Right here now for instance — that man in the gray suit with a heavy gold watch chain looping across his vest; he'd never seen him before. And that fellow with the black whiskers that looked like a nest, standing behind him — a stranger, too. Probably transients. Still, they could be moving in. Town already had one new resident; that Miss — or was it Mrs.? — Keel. Thinking of starting a ladies dress shop —

"You say south, Mayor?"

Lawson snapped back to the moment. "What the sheriff said."

"Sending a posse after him?"

"No. The sheriff says he wants to go in by himself. He's afraid a big party of riders will be seen by the killer. And by the Apaches."

There was a long moment of silence. Someone whistled softly. A voice said: "You mean he's going in there alone — all by himself?"

"What he wants but I can't allow it. I've decided to send a U.S. marshal with him. A few legal problems involved, getting into a different county, maybe another Territory, even. I'm sending off a telegram to the Governor, telling him I want the marshal."

"Be two days at least before he can get here," someone pointed out. "With that much of a start a man could get clean into Mexico."

"Main reason I'm asking for a Federal lawman," Henry said patiently. "I want Sul Rich brought back alive for hanging. Got to let the whole country know we don't put up with that kind of a criminal around here. So, once the sheriff starts after him I don't want anything standing in the way of his bringing him back."

26

"Ain't much chance of you ever getting your hanging," Perry Wold said. "Stranger in the Espantoso's a dead man before he starts across it. If the heat don't get him, the 'Paches sure will."

"Possible," Lawson admitted. "I'm hoping he'll be lucky and stay alive until Guthry and the marshal can track him down. He's one man that's got to hang . . . Now, if you all will excuse me, I'll send that telegram."

He came off the porch, crossed the yard. Entering the street, he bent his steps toward the telegraph office, noting as he did, the slender, nicely dressed figure of Cathren Keel on the steps fronting the hotel. Evidently she had just come down from her room. He nodded pleasantly, continued on his way.

The crowd had swung in behind him. Pleased at that, Lawson struck up a conversation with Pete Akins who was to his left, dwelling further on the importance of bringing Sul Rich back to Lawsonville where he could be made to pay, with suitable Territorial-wide publicity, for his crimes. Men like him must be made to realize that Lawsonville was no hick town, that it wasn't a place where the law could be trifled with. Other criminals would hear of Sul Rich's fate, steer clear of the settlement, you can bet on that.

He reached the telegraph office, again excused himself and went inside. Giving his message to the operator with instructions to ask for an immediate reply, he dallied for a time, and then returned to the street.

"Waiting for my answer," he said before anyone could voice the obvious question, and reached into his pocket for a cigar. Thinking better of that, he diverted the motion of his arm to one of brushing dust from his vest front. He should pass cigars all around, standing there as he was in front of the crowd, but he had only a couple with him. Not good politics. Somebody might think he was slighting the constituency.

Pursing his lips, he looked off down the street. He ought to get busy at putting in the rest of the board sidewalks. There was only about a fifty yard strip left to be done — and sidewalks went over big with the womenfolk. Problem was that there was no money left in the town treasury . . . Might be smart to just advance the cash himself; wouldn't amount to much, and it could pay off big . . . He'd give it some thought.

Ought to look into that railroad business again, too. If they decided to swing down through the valley, he wanted to be the first to know. There was an acre or two of vacant land over on the west side of town that could be bought cheap — not that he'd figure to make any big money on it, but if the land was to be had, a man ought to look ahead a bit.

That's all he'd be doing — looking ahead, and too, he'd be helping the town as a whole. He could take a small chunk of the land, make it into a park across the street from the depot for everybody to use — assuming the railroad did come and they built the depot where he wanted it.

Couple of other things he'd best look into, too. Bridge over Castle Creek needed repairing again. Those damned cattle raisers driving their herds across it — ought to levy a toll on them, so much per head! They were the ones tearing it up all the time . . . But he'd better go easy at first on that, walk sort of soft. Quite a few cattlemen scattered throughout the county, and they swung a lot of influence in the Capital. Moreover, most of them did their trading right there in Lawsonville — and he sure didn't want to run off any business.

Business . . . He glanced toward his own establishment, across the street and down a half block. Should be there looking after his own affairs. Been neglecting things pretty much ever since this Sul Rich mess busted loose. Lucky he had a good, strong wife and four husky sons. They took care of things for him when he got tied up running the town.

"Mr. Mayor —"

Lawson wheeled quickly. Cathren Keel's calm face and cool, gray eyes met his. She was a looker, all right. Wasn't hard to see why she was the first woman Dan Guthry had been known to pay any attention to.

"Yes, Miss Keel?"

"The sheriff — is he going to be all right?"

"Be up and around, good as new in a few days."

She raised her head, stared off into the direction of Borden's office. "And that killer — I understand he got away."

"Yes, he managed that. But don't you worry. We'll have him back here, give him what he's got coming to him before he can harm anybody else . . . Your dress shop — have you decided —"

She gave him a quick smile. "I'm still considering it."

"Fine, fine. I'm sure you'd do real well here —"

"Here's your answer, Henry," the telegraph operator's voice broke in.

Lawson turned to take the message, recalled his manners, wheeled back to excuse himself, but Cathren Keel was already moving off along the walk. He'd remember to apologize to her next time they met. Woman like her, in business of course, would be an asset to the town.

Unfolding the bit of paper with its scrawled message, he read quickly. Frowning, he read it again.

"Well, he coming or ain't he?"

Lawson nodded to the crowd in general. Clearing his throat, he quoted from the reply: "Marshal unavailable from this point at present. Have requested Denver office to dispatch deputy immediately. Have their assurance Deputy Erland Flood leaving today. Arrive your city Friday . . . "

Henry Lawson folded the paper, feeling it unnecessary to further quote the Governor and relate his final words to the effect that Sul Rich had better be caught and punished, or else drastic action on the part of his office would be instigated.

"Means he's not coming on the stage." Gannon's voice carried above the run of conversation. "It ain't due in from the north until Saturday. Only way he can get here by Friday is cut across the mountains, ride down through Horseshoe Pass."

Henry Lawson signified his agreement, neatly turned the moment to its best advantage. "Fine cooperation — from both the Governor and the marshal's office in Denver. Always found it pays to know the right people."

30

There was a faint cheer. Gannon said something in a low voice, spun, headed for Halleran's Saloon. Lawson continued to smile benignly upon the crowd.

"Now, I don't want you folks worrying about anything. You can sleep easy. Your mayor's got this whole nasty business under control — just like you elected him to do. In a week, ten days maybe, we'll have Sul Rich back here in Lawsonville again, this time ready to step up onto the scaffold and pay for his crimes . . . You've got my word on it."

Pay for his crimes!

The gaunt man with the nest of black whiskers and piercing blue eyes noticed earlier by Mayor Lawson as a stranger, allowed those words to trickle through his mind as the crowd ranged around him began to break up, melt into the growing night. Outwardly he was calm, even inoffensive in his appearance, but inwardly all was raging turbulence and torture.

Pay for his crimes!

Those words became as a river of fire burning through his brain, set a great anger welling through him and started his hungry frame to trembling like aspen leaves in a wind.

It was not for them to make James Sullivan Rich pay for his crimes! The Almighty, in the guise of Amos Rich — the parent — the father — the one responsible for James Sullivan Rich's presence on this earth would perform that sacred duty!

No blabbering town mayor, no lawman — sheriff or marshal — would exact the last breath of life from

James Sullivan Rich. The Almighty had spoken — had commanded. The Almighty would be obeyed.

Amos Rich, you have sired an abomination — a sinner. He has killed. He has defiled. I command you to take My vengeance upon him — your son — and rid the earth of his evil self!

That's the way it had come down to him, a shaft of blinding light reaching from the heavens, piercing the layers of darkness, filling him with fear and determination.

"Yes, God," he had answered humbly, and immediately had prepared to set forth from the small starveout farm in Kansas where, alone since the death of his wife Mary, and the disappearance of their son a year or so earlier, he had endeavored to eke out a livelihood.

The word from above, oddly enough, had come to him on the very day he had heard from an itinerant peddler of the murders in a town called Lawsonville, and that the killer, one Sul Rich, had been jailed for the killings. It was some sort of miracle arranged by the Almighty, Amos supposed.

He'd been directed to carry out the Almighty's will, and the Almighty was making it possible, yes, even easy for him to do so. All that was necessary was for him to ride to this Lawsonville, a town in New Mexico Territory, walk into the jail and put a bullet into the head of James Sullivan Rich. Thus the Almighty would be served.

It had taken a few days to get things ready, however. A man had to be hired to drop by, feed the small jag of livestock still on the place; cash had to be raised by selling off a few articles, and as a result, he was late in departing, late in arriving in Lawsonville — too late, in fact. He rode into the settlement with the news of Sul Rich's spectacular escape and additional murders spilling from the lips of everyone.

But the Almighty had imbued him with patience. He'd stood around in the crowds listening to all that was said, taking in all that was to be. It resolved itself finally into one thing; the sheriff, a man named Daniel Guthry, would recover shortly and then, in company with a deputy U.S. marshal by the name of Erland Flood, would set out to track down the killer. The sheriff knew the country into which James Sullivan had fled. Guthry would find him and then he and the marshal would bring James Sullivan Rich back and hang him.

Only it couldn't be that way. The death of James Sullivan Rich must come at the hands of his own father, else the word would not be fulfilled, the stain removed. True justice was the province of the Almighty and a force never to be questioned. Amos Rich had created James Sullivan Rich, therefore it was only right the Almighty, in His infinite wisdom, had decreed that he, Amos Rich, should destroy him.

In the end as in the beginning a man was responsible for his acts in the eyes of the Almighty. *What a man creates, and it be evil, he must then destroy . . . destroy . . . destroy . . . .* It was the law — a mighty law higher than that of mayors and governors and sheriffs.

Amos stood quiet and alone in the darkening street, a slight, bent figure, eyes glowing, out-sized fists opening, clenching, opening. He could not fail. He must not fail. His was the holy charge, the sacred trust, he was the chosen dispenser of high justice. He had failed the Almighty in the creation of James Sullivan, but a second chance, one by which he could redeem himself, had been granted. He would not again fail.

It was to his own shame that he had not recognized the evil forces at work within his son in those first years of life; the cruelty, the lying, the sinning, the vagabond ways. But Mary, the Almighty rest her soul, had prevailed upon him and he had spared the boy. He had been weak.

"Was my sin, O Lord!"

The words ripped involuntarily from his lips, soared out into the darkness. Two men standing in front of Halleran's turned to look, curious as to the outburst, and seeing only the scarecrow figure of an old man they did not know, shortly resumed their conversation.

Elsewhere in Lawsonville he also went unnoticed. The evening was getting under way. Music was seeping from the saloons; the bell of the Methodist Church was summoning the faithful to prayer. Somewhere down the street an anvil rang in clear, sweet tones as a blacksmith worked late at his trade.

Horseshoe Pass . . . The key to the situation came to Amos Rich almost with the speed and lucidity of the Almighty's first message . . . Go there . . . Wait . . . and when Erland Flood came by, strike swiftly . . . No need to kill, simply remove him, tie him up, leave him where

34

he'd not be found for a few days — and assume his identity.

He would then become the new Deputy U.S. Marshal Erland Flood sent to accompany Sheriff Guthry, and as such the success of his sacred trust would be assured.

Alone, in the darkness of her room, Cathren Keel looked down on the deserted street. It was very late and the only lights were in the saloons, and one in the doctor's office . . . Probably at Dan Guthry's bedside.

Restless, disappointed, she had been unable to sleep, had spent most of the evening's latter part pacing the floor. How long, really, would it take Dan Guthry and the U.S. marshal they'd sent for, to bring Rich back — *ready to step up onto the scaffold*, as the mayor had put it? A week or ten days had been his estimate, but Cathren had her doubts.

They didn't know Rich as she did. They didn't know how cunning and clever — and how tricky he could be. A dozen times he had reached the end of his rope and then, as if by magic — but maybe it would be different here. Guthry wasn't the sort of man who'd sidetrack easily, or who would ever give up.

They were alike in that respect, Cathren thought; she'd never give up on Rich either — and this time she had been within a step of bringing an end to the quest that had set her to roaming the country — only to have him slip through her fingers once again . . . It was frustrating and disappointing and difficult to accept, being so close and yet again losing; but, as before, she faced failure philosophically ... If Guthry and the marshal didn't bring him back, then she would simply resume the search ... And someday, somewhere, luck would favor her; she'd not be too late, and she'd settle her score with this man they were calling Sul Rich.

CHAPTER
FIVE

Deputy Marshal Flood arrived in Lawsonville in the mid-afternoon of that Friday. He entered Main Street, rode directly down center until he reached the sheriff's office, and there pulled up to the hitchrack.

Inside the heat laden frame structure Dan Guthry, slumped in his chair, had impatiently waited out an irritating day. Physically, he felt in fine fettle once again. The wound in his arm and the one on the side of his head had been no more than severe cuts causing loss of blood and a degree of shock, according to Doc Borden. But the medical man wasn't guaranteeing anything insofar as those raps on the skull were concerned — he'd made that amply clear to Dan as well as to Mayor Lawson. There could be some sort of delayed reaction.

Guthry had brushed off the warning. The two days treatment and rest combined with good food liberally laced with whiskey had put him on his feet. Now, troubled by no more than a slight stiffness in the arm and a gnawing sensation on the side of the head where a scab had formed, he was anxious to move out after Sul Rich.

It was the waiting for Marshal Flood that almost got him down. Alone most of the time, as was his habit, he had done considerable thinking, and during those hours he had been unable to shake the inner conviction of disgrace — and injured pride — that the loss of his prisoner had engendered, extenuating circumstances notwithstanding.

In his own mind was the sense of failure. He should have used more care, he continually told himself; he should have been more alert, expected the unexpected.

The escape was a scar on his record — a defeat that galled him to rawness and tarnished the fine job he had done in Lawsonville, which had been exceptionally free of crime since he'd pinned on the star.

Sul Rich had wiped all that out — all the hard work, the careful intent with which he'd done his job, the faith so painstakingly built within people. And the only hope he had of restoring himself to any extent in the eyes of others, according to his way of thinking, was to bring Sul Rich back alive.

Such wouldn't return to life the persons who were dead, of course. The toll was up to five now; the second juror had died; but hanging Sul Rich would be some compensation and perhaps would make everyone, including himself, feel a little better.

No one blamed him at least vocally for what had taken place. But Dan Guthry imagined he saw it in some with whom he spoke — excepting, maybe, Cathren Keel, who, in that calm, quiet way of hers, appeared to hold no opinions at all on the matter. But he thought he detected it in others — in the way they avoided mentioning the matter, in the carefully clothed accusation lying deep in their eyes — and had mentioned it to Henry Lawson. The mayor had promptly assured him there was nothing to it, that it was, in fact, pure imagination.

Nobody faulted him for what had occurred, Lawson said. It was just one of those things — a black mark against the town, sure, and a thing that had to be rectified quickly by the capture and punishment of the killer. But he needn't worry. His job was safe — leastwise it was as long as he, Henry Lawson, had any say.

Job be damned! That wasn't what chewed so persistently at his vitals! He'd let it happen. Indirectly, he had permitted the deaths of three of the five Sul Rich had murdered — and that fact would live with him for a long time to come.

Maybe the answer was to give up lawing, turn in his badge, look for some other kind of work. Ranch foreman, trail boss, plain cowpuncher, he could do any of those, and he'd be getting completely away from wearing a star.

He'd thought a little about it back there in that sandy coulee where Sul Rich had dumped him, and he was considering it again . . . He just might do it once he'd brought in the killer and the mess was cleaned up.

Such considerations had plagued him continually since he had regained full control of his senses that morning after Gannon and the others had brought him in to Borden's office. Lawson's subsequent advice that he had sent for a U.S. marshal to aid in the recapture of the killer hadn't improved matters any . . . He didn't need help, didn't want any — and what was worse, that action on the part of the mayor seemed to prove that a loss of confidence was involved.

And the waiting — the delay in getting started; that was bad, served only to further whet the impatience that boiled through him and sharpen the edge of his temper. Thus, when finally he saw the Federal lawman pull up in front of his office, he was on his feet in an instant and moving to the doorway.

He halted in the opening, leaned against the frame, and with subconscious hostility, surveyed the man. Flood was older than he had expected. Not tall, and lean to the point of being cadaverous. He had a narrow, sunken face that bore a pink glow as if freshly shaved and then bared to the sun.

His eyes, deep pocketed beneath frayed, sandy brows, were a piercing blue and closely set to a thin nose with narrow nostrils that overhung a wide mouth filled with broad, somewhat stained teeth.

He wore a flat crowned hat, low heeled Hyer boots, corded breeches that appeared a bit too large for him. The buckskin jacket he sported was fringed to aid in draining off water during a heavy rainstorm — something, Guthry thought humorlessly, he'd have no need for in the powder dry bottoms and scorched flats of the Espantoso.

Dan remained silent, allowed the older man to sweep him with his critical glance, also make his assessment and draw his conclusions. When it was done he stepped out onto the small landing.

"Marshal Flood?"

The lawman nodded, came forward onto the planks, his over-large hands with their thick, stubby fingers hanging motionless at his sides.

"That's me," he said in a strong midwest twang, "you the sheriff?"

With the star pinned to the pocket of his shirt the question seemed pointless to Guthry, but he bobbed his head. "Guthry's the name. Come in out of the sun."

He drew back into the office, noting the figure of Henry Lawson hurrying up from across the street. Flood walked stiffly into the room, removed his hat, brushed at the accumulation of sweat on his tortured looking face.

"We ready to pull out?"

Faint surprise stirred Guthry. He had expected the marshal would want to lay over the night, rest, get an early start in the morning. Evidently Flood shared his own anxiety to get on the killer's trail.

"Any time you say."

Henry Lawson appeared in the doorway, best political smile parting his lips. Extending his hand, he bustled forward.

"Marshal Flood? Pleasure to welcome you — and thank you for your help. You made good time. I'm Henry Lawson, mayor here — of Lawsonville."

The marshal shook hands gravely, acknowledged it all with only faint movement of his hard, drilling eyes. He was not going to be much for small talk, Dan guessed, and was pleased with the thought.

"Expect your office filled you in on the details concerning our problem," Lawson continued. "The sheriff —"

"Reckon I know all I'm needing to know," Flood broke in.

"Good. Might add that the other man Rich shot died. Makes it five he killed."

The lawman digested that bit of information, stared off toward the hills beyond the town. "Evil begets evil," he murmured.

"How was that?" Lawson asked.

Erland Flood shrugged. "Terrible thing. Man like that running loose. Was just asking the sheriff how soon we could start. Important I — we get right after the killer."

"My feelings exactly. Well, expect you can leave any time you decide," Lawson said, glancing at Guthry.

"Pulling out now," Dan said, and then to Flood: "You'll need a fresh horse."

The marshal only nodded. Guthry moved to the door, shouted to the hostler lounging in front of Hammind's Livery Stable.

"Billy, come get this horse," and when the elderly man had crossed over, gave added instructions as to what he wanted done as well as ordering his own sorrel made ready for the trail.

Behind him Henry Lawson was asking, half apologetically, to see Flood's credentials. The lawman dug into an inside pocket of his buckskin jacket, produced a leather fold of papers which he passed to the mayor. Lawson examined them hastily, returned them.

"Formality, you understand," he said. "Been a rule of mine to always keep things on a business basis." Turning to Dan he asked, "Everything all set?"

"Horses'll be ready in a few minutes. Got grub and water together this morning. We won't —"

"Like for you to know we think a lot of our sheriff, Marshal," Lawson interrupted, swinging back to face Flood. "Proud to say he's the best in the Territory. Had no trouble around here at all until these killings — and that was no fault of his. No, sir, not at all."

Flood's face was impassive. Only his eyes, glowing and restless in their recessed niches, seemed alive.

"Was about to say," Guthry continued, irritated by Lawson's interruption, "we'll be traveling without a pack horse. Figure it would slow us down too much. We'll carry everything we need."

"You think that smart?" Lawson asked doubtfully. "Hunt could stretch into several days — even weeks."

"Probably will. But time's something we're up against. Got to make up all we can. Taking two canteens of water apiece — that's the main thing. Having to trim our own grub supply a little so's we can take grain for the horses. Damned little grazing in the Espantoso."

"Well, you're familiar with that country," Lawson said. "Expect you know what you're doing." He turned again to the marshal. "Sheriff Guthry's one of the few men who know the Espantoso — that's the area you'll be heading into."

Flood remained silent, his gaze now on the gun rack behind Guthry's desk.

"Be obliged for the loan of a rifle and some cartridges," he said, making no move to select one of the weapons. "Come off in such a hurry, forgot mine."

Guthry glanced at the worn-handled pistol slung against the lawman's leg. A long range weapon would come in handy, he reckoned.

"Take your pick," he said, stepping forward and keying the padlock to release the chain.

Flood scanned the half a dozen rifles, chose a Winchester carbine. Guthry handed him a box of ammunition from the stack on the shelf, then selecting an earlier model, Henry, because of his familiarity with it, restored the chain.

Outside in the street the slow thud of hooves intermingling with a quick rumble of talk announced the arrival of the horses. Word had gotten around fast of the impending departure of the lawmen, and a crowd was gathering. Guthry bucked his head at Flood.

"Expect we're ready."

For reply the marshal clamped his hat on his head, and hanging the Winchester in the crook of his arm, started for the doorway.

"Good luck," Lawson said brightly, and then as Guthry passed by, caught at his arm. "You've got to bring Rich in alive, Dan, remember that. Important we hang him."

Guthry's shoulders stirred. "He'll be alive — if he'll come that way."

"Governor's not going to be satisfied otherwise."

"Maybe it ought to be the Governor riding down into the Espantoso after him," Dan said dryly.

"I only mean —"

"Don't fret over it. I want to see Rich swing from a scaffold as much as you and the Governor do, but don't bank too strong on it. Sul Rich's got everything to lose and nothing to gain. He's not going to just stand still, let me slap the irons on him without a fight."

"Of course — of course! Don't take any chances. Only, if it's possible —"

Guthry again shrugged, followed Flood into the street. The marshal was waiting, paying no mind to the crowd gathered in the driving sunlight anxious for a look at the Federal lawman and to witness the start of the hunt for Sul Rich. He raised his brows inquiringly at Dan. Guthry pointed to the strong black he'd chosen for the lawman, knowing the horse had plenty of bottom and could stand the hard trip that lay ahead.

Flood booted his rifle, swung to the saddle, settled himself. Dan mounted his sorrel, jammed the Henry into leather, and made a quick, visual check of equipment to be certain the hostler had forgotten nothing. Satisfied, he pulled away from the rail.

"Hope you catch him, Sheriff," a voice called from the crowd.

Guthry nodded unsmilingly as Flood curved his black in abreast the sorrel. He glanced toward the hotel — to where the slender figure of Cathren Keel stood on the porch. She was wearing a pale blue dress of cool looking material, and the sight of her waiting there to see him off stirred him far deeper than he thought possible.

As they passed the hotel she lifted her hand in a silent farewell, smiled faintly. Guthry nodded, touched the brim of his hat with a forefinger. He hoped she would still be in Lawsonville when he returned.

CHAPTER
SIX

In silence the two men reached the last of the houses, broke out onto the flat that stretched, brown and lifeless, to the south. There, Flood shifted heavily on his saddle.

"Where was it you come close to getting killed? Like to have a look at the spot."

It was a request that made little sense to Dan Guthry, but he altered course slightly so as to pass the coulee. He had planned to line out directly south, pick up the trail Sul Rich would have followed somewhat farther on. But a mile or so out of the way would probably matter little — and Erland Flood undoubtedly had his reasons.

"Right here," he said a time later when they drew up to the rim of the sandy swale. "Rich headed off that direction," he added, pointing. "Tracks are gone now."

The marshal stared mutely at the scuff marks in the soil, the trampled weeds where a horse had stood, his expression vacant, non-revealing. What he was getting out of it Guthry could not imagine — and they were wasting time. No amount of staring at the ground would put them any nearer to Sul Rich.

Wordless, he touched the sorrel with his spurs, moved off along the route taken by the fleeing killer. A minute afterwards he heard the thud of Flood's black coming up behind him, guessed the lawman had satisfied whatever it was that had bothered him.

"There any other place James Sullivan could go?"

Guthry looked at the lawman blankly. "Who?"

Flood rubbed at his jaw. "James Sullivan Rich. That's his full name," he said, and then as an afterthought, added: "Got it from the papers."

"Called himself Sul Rich while he was around here. You know him from times before?"

"Heard of him . . . Any towns ahead of us?"

"Not for close onto a hundred miles."

"Recollect you mentioning somebody name of Maxwell. Thought maybe that was a settlement."

Dan couldn't remember it coming up but apparently it had. "Maxwell's a homesteader. Lives with his wife and boy on a little place this side of the Espantoso. Figure to refill our canteens there, water the horses. Can pick up some fresh grub too, if we need it."

"Espantoso," Flood repeated absently. "It mean something?"

"Mexican word. Means a frightful place — or maybe fearful would say it better. Big sink country."

"And you figure Rich went into it?"

"Had to. No way around it when you're this close. Don't think he knew what he was riding into, else he'd have picked another direction at the start."

"Why's that?"

"Name means just what it says. Nothing but desert. No water anywhere. All you'll find for days are snakes, cactus, scorpions, and heat that climbs up over a hundred. That and some real unfriendly Apaches."

"Indians — living in a place like that?"

"Along the edges, mostly. But it counts with them. Sort of like a private land they don't want the whites or the Mexicans fooling around in. *El hogar de muerte*, they call it — the home of death. Fits it perfect."

"That mayor fellow said you'd been there. Seems you had no trouble."

"Pa was a mining man. Traipsed around after him for quite a few years when I was a kid. We crossed the Espantoso a dozen times, I expect. He knew it — and how to keep alive in it."

"Must've been a friend of the Indians."

"No, not 'specially. We just dodged them, kept out of sight when they were on the prowl. Learned a lot about things like that from him, along with making myself acquainted with the Espantoso. No place for a man who doesn't know —"

"He'll make it through all right," Flood said, his brooding gaze on the distant skyline.

"You're talking about Sul Rich?"

The marshal nodded. Guthry considered the statement in silence as the horses plodded steadily on. The sun was sliding toward the ragged line of hills to the west and the heat was breaking a little. It would be a welcome relief.

"What makes you so sure?"

"Satan always takes care of his own, while the faithful sometimes perish . . . Never could rightly understand that but the ways of the Almighty are strange — and not to be questioned . . . All have purpose."

Guthry stared at the older man. He rode hunched over his saddle, still wore the fringed buskskin despite the wilting temperature.

"But reckoning comes. Enemies of the Almighty face their penalty. They pay — if not by His hand by that of someone chosen by Him."

Who the hell was he riding with? A preacher? Some hallelujah-shouting soul saver? Dan wondered. He was hearing odd words from the lips of a lawman — but maybe not. Men did become imbued with the fires of righteousness and the need to serve their God. Nothing exempted a lawman from such or ruled it impossible. Still . . .

"How long've you been a marshal?" Dan asked, reaching for his cigarette makings.

Flood stirred. "Not long."

"You wear another badge before that — a sheriff or something?"

"Was a farmer. Worked the land, up Kansas way."

That explained the hands, the thick fingers that would have difficulty in slipping swiftly inside the trigger guard of a pistol. The preference for a rifle was clear now, as was an earlier hunch that Flood hadn't been a U.S. marshal for any great length of time. He shifted restlessly. Erland Flood could prove to be more a hindrance than a help. He wished now he'd ignored

Lawson's wishes, gone on alone. But it was too late now to do anything about that.

Curious, and thinking of Flood's words, he said: "You really believe that about a man like Sul Rich always getting what's coming to him? Can think of a few outlaws still running loose."

"Their time will come — their hour of judgment. If not by the hand of the Almighty — by His agent."

"Agent . . . You figure you're one?"

"I do. The word came down to me plain. Told me it was my duty. I understood — and I got to obey."

Dan wagged his head. "I've been a lawman for quite a spell, and I sure don't remember ever getting any special word about outlaws."

"Reckon it don't come to all men. Just them the Almighty figures is strong enough to do what they're told. Takes strength to carry out the Almighty's vengeance sometimes."

Guthry sucked at a dead cigarette. Flood was a strange one, no doubt of that. But he must be an able lawman; he'd not be wearing the star of a deputy U.S. marshal if he weren't. Uncomfortable and disturbed by his thoughts of the future, he looked ahead gloomily.

The land was breaking up, becoming rougher and much wilder. The flat across which they had ridden was giving way to countless arroyos, sand filled and overgrown with greasewood, snakeweed and rabbitbrush. Cholla and prickly pear cactus scarred the slopes, and here and there a stunted cedar spread thinly needled branches upward as if beseeching rain.

He raised his gaze to the west. Dark was a couple of hours off. That should put them close to Pinto Buttes. Be a good place to camp for the night. No point in trying to go too far. Flood was beat, he could see that. Get a good night's rest and push hard tomorrow.

"When'll we get to the Maxwell place?" the old lawman wondered.

"Tomorrow sometime — probably late. Figured we'd best make camp about sundown. Be hard going after today." Guthry paused, added: "Expect you could use some rest. Ride down from Denver's no Sunday picnic."

"The Almighty gives me strength," Erland Flood intoned, and lapsed again into a moody quiet.

CHAPTER
SEVEN

They rose in that hushed, lonely hour before daylight. Guthry got a fire going, set a lard tin of water over it for coffee, and digging out a blackened spider and their provisions, began to prepare breakfast.

Flood, morose and tight-lipped, worked at readying the horses for the coming day. No words passed between them, some unspoken understanding prompting each to assume a share of the necessary duties.

The marshal, finished with his chores, and seeing the meal was not as yet ready, dug into his gear and procured soap and razor, and moved up close to the fire. Only then was the silence broken.

"Be smart to leave those whiskers," Guthry said. "Sun'll be hell from here on."

The older man stared thoughtfully into the flames as if not convinced. Dan watched him from the tail of an eye for a moment and then shrugging indifferently, turned back to stirring the strips of bacon and chunks of potatoes sizzling in the frying pan.

"Face of yours looks like it could stand a rest from a blade," he observed. "Almost raw. Must not be much sunshine up Colorado way."

Flood grunted an unintelligible reply but he wheeled and restored his shaving equipment to its place inside his saddlebags. The food was ready shortly after, plentiful and calculated to stay with them until the end of the day. There would be no halting to salve hunger this side of the Maxwells'.

The quiet continued to hang between them, not necessarily one of anger or resentment, but simply an attitude of reserve wherein words had no place and only thought and motion were of consequence.

A short time later they were again in the saddle, bearing now somewhat to the southwest. The country maintained its rugged characteristics, but now a gradual sloping had taken over, as if the land had suddenly decided to slant downward into some distant pit. And pit it would be, Dan thought wryly. The Espantoso in August — a man as well bargain to ride across hell with all its fires ablaze; the punishment would be no less.

Little stirred on the gray, scorched earth. A lizard now and then appeared, already panting from the relentlessly rising heat, to stare at them in their passage. A lone jack-rabbit, tall, black tipped ears stiffly erect, bounded off through the starved growth. Vultures were in the sky, already searching the land below for prey as they soared effortlessly in broad, sweeping circles. Dan Guthry's jaw tightened at the sight of the great, poised shadows. He hated them more than ever now, the recollection of his brush with them still fresh in mind.

On toward noon they halted to rest the horses and ease their own aching muscles in a skimpy strip of shade at the foot of a bluff. Swinging down stiff-kneed, Flood stood for a time chafing the insides of his thighs while he squinted across the blistered world shimmering before them.

"How much more of this 'til we reach the Maxwell place?"

"Five, maybe six hours," Dan replied, unhooking one of the canteens. He recalled imparting similar information to the lawman only the day before. Flood's memory apparently wasn't too good.

Reaching into a saddle pocket, he obtained a rag, saturated it with water and squeezed it dry into the mouth of the sorrel. Finished, he glanced at Flood. The lawman had made no such move to care for the black. Wadding the rag into a ball, he tossed it to Flood.

"Better water that horse," he said. "Man looks after his animal down here or he finds himself afoot."

The marshal merely nodded, went through the chore. It done, he returned the cloth, said: "You figure there's a chance Rich'll still be at the Maxwells'?"

That thought had entered Guthry's mind earlier. Maxwell's would be a good place for a man to lay over, but he doubted Sul Rich would take advantage of the homesteader's hospitality for any length of time. Too much lay behind him. His primary thought would be to get out of the country as fast as possible, once he was set to travel. And he'd know that Maxwell's was only a long day's ride from Lawsonville.

"Maybe," he said, now slacking off on the saddle cinches to further relieve his horse. "My guess is he stayed a day, moved on."

Flood nodded, studied Guthry closely. "Seems you come to know him pretty well."

"Not much. Know his kind and what they'll usually do when the law's pushing them."

"He talk much while you had him locked up waiting for the trial?"

"Some. Mostly bragging. About the things he'd done, the women he'd had — stuff like that."

"Was born bad," the marshal said. "Bad blood from the beginning. Like an outlaw horse —"

"No man's born mean, same as no horse is," Dan said. "He just gets that way. Something turns him, brings it on. Same goes for any animal. They're all right when they're new dropped. It's what happens to them later that makes them bad."

"Wrong!" Erland Flood contradicted flatly. "Not like that at all. Bad blood, through and through. Like as if the devil was born right in them."

Guthry shrugged, unwilling to argue the point. It was too hot and there would be too many days of close association ahead to allow enmity to spring up between them. Damned foolish argument, anyway.

A half hour later they were once more in the saddle, bearing due west now to where the land appeared to be leveling off. To the south it continued its gradual sliding away. Soon they were entering a long peninsula that speared out to rise above the Espantoso and form an overlooking bluff. The Maxwell place stood near its tip.

They'd reach the homesteader's a bit earlier than he'd expected, Dan realized. That was a comforting thought. A good night's rest in pleasant quarters before tackling the trails of the Espantoso was something he could use. For one thing, Doc Borden had been partly right; his head was throbbing dully and a soreness had developed in the arm where Rich's bullet had ripped its bloody path.

He'd have a look at it when they stopped. Perhaps Mrs. Maxwell would have something he could put on the wound, relieve what likely was inflammation. Homesteader's wives, living at the ends of nowhere, were resourceful souls, always seemingly able to handle such things.

By mid-afternoon, sweat soaking them, horses lathered and showing strain from the steady push, they came in sight of the Maxwell holdings — a gray, green, irregular blotch on the otherwise brown landscape. It was too distant to make out the buildings, but the tiny oasis was evident by its different color, occasioned by the trees and small fields under cultivation.

Maxwell had a deep, painstakingly dug well that flowed strong and clear year in and year out. It furnished not only ample water for the family's personal and farm use, but supplied any passerby as well — and welcome.

"Can see the place pretty good now," Erland Flood said when they had drawn nearer — and breaking what had been another lengthy silence. "That an apple orchard he's got?"

Dan brushed sweat from his face, grunted in surprise. The marshal knew his farming; the trees were certainly too far away for him to make any such distinction, had he not already known.

"What it is. Maxwell picks up a little side money to help keep things going by selling apples in town during the season. How could you tell from here?"

"Way the trees grow — and the planting's done," Flood said, and offered no more explanation.

With the passage of another half hour they reached the fringe of the Maxwell fields and were in a narrow lane that led between adjacent rows of corn standing ripe and still in the hot, motionless air.

A quiet possessed the place, a hush that registered finally upon Dan Guthry, brought him to a halt some distance short of the adobe structures that made up the farm and were as yet not visible to them.

"What're we stopping here for?" Flood demanded, easing himself on the saddle by rising slightly.

"Something wrong," Guthry replied in a low voice. "Ought to be hearing things. Dog ought to be barking." Reaching down he drew his pistol. "Best we move in slow."

Holding the horses to a quiet walk, they continued down the narrow roadway. Reaching its end, they broke out onto the hard packed yard. A dozen vultures instantly sprang into flight, their powerful wings fanning the dead air into hot wind as they wheeled off toward the orchard to settle in the trees.

"Somebody laying there on the ground — near the house," Flood said, matter-of-factly. "Dog, too."

Guthry nodded, fighting a heavy sickness in the pit of his stomach. The bloated, mangled shape near the house was not the only one; another lay near the

58

chicken yard; a third, considerably smaller, was in the doorway of the barn. The buzzards had been at all.

Pulling his bandana over his nose and mouth to stifle the stench, Guthry spurred forward. Flood's voice caught at him.

"Careful! Could be whoever's done this is still around."

Dan brushed the warning aside. "Damned buzzards wouldn't be here then," he said.

Reaching the figure by the house, he came off the saddle, hung there briefly as horror and disgust rolled through him. It was — or had been — Rafe Maxwell. The vultures had ripped his body to shreds.

"Woman over here," Flood called from the pen where a dozen or more chickens scrambled and clamored anxiously for a feeding. "Reckon she's Maxwell's wife. Can't hardly tell much about anything."

Dan crossed to where the lawman stood waving at the hordes of buzzing flies with his hat. "Mrs. Maxwell, all right," he said.

Stiff, bandana clutched to his face, he continued to where the third figure lay. A young Mexican boy, twelve, perhaps thirteen years old. The vultures hadn't gotten at him to any extent as yet. There were two bullet holes between his small shoulders.

Flood came up, halted, looked close at the boy. "That the son?"

Dan shook his head. "Somebody they took in, gave a home, probably. Were that kind of folks. Look inside the barn. Lot — that's the son — may be in there. He'd be grown by now."

"Where you going?"

"Into the house, see if he's there. Or around the back."

They could find no sign of Lot Maxwell. It was evident he had not been on the premises when the killings occurred.

"You reckon it was the Indians?" Flood asked. "Looks like their kind of doing."

"No, not them," Dan replied. "They'd have burned everything to the ground before they left. And they'd not waste bullets on a kid."

The marshal scrubbed at the sweat on his chin. "Then I expect you're figuring it was Rich."

"I am. The kind of killing he'd do — crazy, useless nosense sort of thing. Like a weasel — kill just for the hell of killing." He paused, looked off toward the fields. "Nothing we can do but bury them. Shovels'll be in the barn."

There was something else in the low roofed, shadowy structure — an empty pistol still containing exploded shell casings. Apparently tossed aside when empty, it caught Guthry's attention as he searched for a spade. Picking it up, he examined it closely.

"Guess this proves it was Rich," he said, beckoning to Flood. "My gun — the one he took off me. Used up the cartridges, threw it away. Other pistol of his must be a different caliber."

Flood sighed heavily, leaned upon the long handled shovel he'd chosen. "Just can't understand how one man can hold so much evil," he said, and turned for the door.

The buzzards had ventured in again, edging nearer in ungainly strides. Angrily Guthry drew his pistol, fired two quick shots into their midst, sending them leaping upward in noisy flaps and soaring off once more for the orchard.

They dug the graves in a small clearing behind the house, and then wrapping the desecrated bodies in blankets, lowered them into the ground and covered them over. The dog they dragged into a shallow trench, filled it in also.

"Ought to be markers," Flood said.

Guthry searched about for a length of board, broke it into three pieces. Taking a bullet from his cartridge belt, he wrote RAFE on one, MRS. MAXWELL on the second, and MEXICAN BOY on the third.

"Best I leave a note for Lot, too, telling him what we found," he said, thrusting the markers into the proper mounds of freshly turned soil. "He'll need to know."

"We don't know what happened — exactly," Flood said.

"We do — near enough."

The marshal shrugged. "Yeh, reckon so . . . When you figure the killings took place?" he said as they moved back toward the house.

"Yesterday sometime. Likely in the afternoon, judging from the bodies. That what you'd guess?"

"What I was thinking," Flood said, agreeing quickly. "That'd mean the man who done it is only a day ahead of us, if he held up for night."

Dan looked off into the south. The Espantoso, only partly visible because of the trees and the growing corn, lay in a colorless haze of late afternoon heat.

"A day — no more than that. If the horses were in better shape —"

"Seen a couple in the barn."

"Work stock. Be too slow. Better off to use our own. Best thing we can do, anyway, is rest up here tonight, get an early start."

Flood seemed anxious to press on. "Might be a better idea to keep going, make it far as we can, then pull up. Be that much closer to him."

It was the first conflict of opinions insofar as the search was concerned — one that could resolve itself into a test of authority. Erland Flood was the senior lawman, but Guthry knew the country — and Rich was his escaped prisoner.

"Hardly worth it," he said quietly. "Horses'll need good care for what's ahead of them. Spending the night in Maxwell's barn with plenty of fresh hay, grain and water will set them up in fine shape. Same idea goes for us. We stay here."

"But all the time he's pulling away —"

Dan Guthry mopped wearily at his eyes. "Rich isn't going anywhere very fast — not down in the Espantoso —"

Abruptly he halted. His hand dropped swiftly to the pistol on his hip. A man was standing in the yard.

CHAPTER
EIGHT

"Indian?" Flood murmured, seeing the dark face.

"Mexican," Guthry replied, allowing his hand to slide on by his weapon when he saw the man was not armed.

"*Quien es usted?*"

The Mexican inclined his head slightly at the lawman's question. "Juan Severo, a herder of goats," he answered gravely, also in Spanish. "You are the law. Is something the matter?"

"You live here?"

"No, in a small camp to the east. The old gentleman and his lady are good friends. Where are they, please?"

Guthry studied the elderly man for a moment. Then: "There was trouble. Both are dead."

"Dead! How is this?"

"By the hand of an assassin."

"Assassin! Tell me. There was a boy. Mexican, as I myself am. Have you seen him?"

"One of twelve, perhaps thirteen years?"

"Yes, but only ten and big for his years. My grandson. Have you seen him?"

Dan looked away. Juan Severo moved an anxious step closer. "He also —"

Guthry nodded. "I am sorry, old one," he said and pointed to the graves.

Severo wilted. His seamed face appeared to shrink and a sickness came into his dark eyes as a spasm of grief shook him.

"Here he was safe," he murmured. "Here he was with good friends, had for himself a home such as I or his mother had never known. Yet he is now dead. Why is it so?"

"There is no one to answer that."

Flood mopped at his sweaty features. "What's he talking about?"

"Boy was his grandson. Guess he's the only relative."

"He know anything about what happened?"

"No — unless —" Dan hesitated, swung his attention to Severo. "You were here yesterday?"

The elderly man shook his head woodenly. "The day ahead of it. I come not often. It is a long walk. But this week I have come twice to visit."

"Was there a stranger here, one you did not know?"

Severo's eyes were thoughtful. "Yes, a stranger. One with reddish hair and a mouth of cruelty. Is it possible that he —"

"We do not know," Dan said. "We search for an assassin. The man you describe appears to be him. When last did you see him?"

"The day ahead of yesterday. The afternoon. With the coming of night I returned to my goats."

"You do not know the name of this man?"

"It was not given me. A friend of the old gentleman's and his lady, I assumed."

64

Guthry turned to Flood. "Rich was here all right. Severo saw him late the day before yesterday. Probably killed the Maxwells and the boy the next morning, and then rode on."

The marshal looked off toward the Espantoso. "Still figure it'd be smart to keep right after him."

"We'll be needing those horses bad a few days from now. Smarter to keep them in good shape." Guthry's tone was short, bore the implication of finality insofar as that particular matter was concerned.

Erland Flood's eyes snapped and a moment of truth again seemed imminent, but Juan Severo broke the tension by stepping closer.

"Tell me, please. The boy, was it a death of much suffering? I must know this."

"He died quickly, with no feeling of pain."

"Ah, if it had to be I thank the Virgin that it came so. The young do not bear pain well."

"True . . . There is a son of the Maxwells. Of the name of Lot. He is not here. Why is that?"

Severo's old eyes were on the graves. He appeared not to hear. Dan touched his shoulder, repeated the question. The Mexican nodded.

"Yes, a son. He visits with friends in a distant place. He was expected to return this day, or perhaps it is tomorrow. I do not recall the exactness. A terrible grief now awaits him." Severo paused and a bitterness came over him. "Also there will be terrible anger such as now grows within me. He will seek revenge, and I —"

"What's he saying?" Flood demanded, noting the agitation in Severo's manner.

"Maxwell's son's been away. Looks for him in today, maybe tomorrow. He says Lot'll be out for revenge. Getting the same idea himself."

"You tell him to forget that!" Flood shouted the words. "I — we'll take care of Rich. I don't want them getting underfoot. You tell him that!"

Guthry couched the marshal's words in the more formal, stilted manner of Spanish. "My partner who is a lawman of the Government, says it will be wrong for you and Lot Maxwell to seek revenge. You must not fear. We will find the assassin and he will hang for the wrong he has done."

Severo made no answer, simply stared, unseeing, at Guthry from his dark eyes. Finally he said, "It is the right of a kinsman to take vengeance. The boy was my grandson."

"True, but the law is stronger than the right of kinsmen. I know the ways of your people. I respect and honor them. But you must not interfere with the law of the United States. It is above all."

"It is gringo law of which you speak."

"It is the law of this land which no longer is a part of Mexico. This you must not forget."

"I forget nothing," Juan Severo said quietly. "Do you go now to seek this assassin?"

"In the morning. Our horses have need for rest and feed. Also, I will talk with Lot Maxwell when he comes."

"He may not come this day."

"Then you will tell him what has happened to his people . . . Will you now help us with the horses? Also, the Maxwell livestock is in need of care."

Dan's hope was to switch the older man's thoughts to different channels, away from his grandson, away from a desire for vengeance. He had no wish for Severo and Lot Maxwell to become searching guns also in quest of Sul Rich.

"No," the old Mexican said flatly. "I will sit with my grandson."

Abruptly he moved off, walking stiff and proudly erect toward the graves.

"What's he up to?" Flood asked, suspiciously.

"Nothing much. Wants to be with his grandson. Tried to get him to help with the stock but he turned me down." Dan's eyes followed the slender figure as it made its way into the shadows of the trees. "Expect we'll have trouble."

"From him? How?"

"Likely won't let this pass — and he probably knows the Espantoso better than anybody around, barring the Apaches. Certainly better than me. He takes a notion to head out, beat us to Sul Rich, chances are good he will."

"Then we'll tie him up, fix it so's he can't."

"No need — yet. He'll wait for Lot, maybe team up with him. But we'd best keep an eye on him anyway."

Guthry turned to the sorrel. Taking up the reins he led the horse to the barn. Flood followed suit and for the next hour or so they worked over their mounts, stripping, rubbing them down with feed sacks, and

67

finally treating them to fresh hay, a quantity of oats and water.

When they returned to the yard Juan Severo still crouched by the side of the smallest grave, hunched, hands clasped, elbows resting on his knees.

Guthry dropped his blanket roll beneath a small cottonwood at the edge of the yard. He had no desire now to sleep inside the house where he could enjoy the luxury of a bed, nor did he wish to make use of the Maxwells' kitchen in preparing the evening meal. Somehow it didn't seem right to take advantage of their hospitality with them lying so close by in their graves.

"You like," Erland Flood said, dropping his roll next to Guthry's, "I'll tend the stock while you throw some grub together."

Dan nodded. "Suit yourself."

The marshal moved off, rounded shoulders slack under the buckskin jacket, flat heeled boots spurting up small puffs of powdery dust at each footfall. In the pen the chickens were setting up a noisy racket, scrambling for their ration of feed, and somewhere back of the barn hogs were squealing.

Gathering an armload of dry branches and other litter, Guthry laid his fire and dug out their supply of food and cooking utensils for the preparation of the meal. He'd planned to buy fresh, green items from the Maxwells but that was out now, unless Lot returned before they were ready to depart. They would fill their canteens, however; there'd be nothing wrong in that. Rafe Maxwell's water well was available to anyone in need of that most precious of commodities in the desert.

Three more killings to Sul Rich's credit . . .

That fact drummed through his mind as he got the supper underway. Eight so far that he knew of. How many before he'd made his appearance at the Parsons place? Another eight? Likely even more. Sul Rich was a killer utterly and wholly devoid of conscience and remorse — of compassion in its minutest degree.

Murdering the Maxwells had been a senseless act. He could have had anything they possessed, and taken it with no more than a threat of force, for they were that sort of people — gentle — kind . . . And the boy — shot twice in the back as he apparently had fled, terror stricken, for the safety of the barn. Why would he kill a small boy? What devious reasoning could lie behind that savage, inhuman deed?

No reason at all. Only a blind, lusting hunger to kill — to destroy. No matter the cause — none was necessary. Simply kill — end a life. The determination to drag Rich back to the gallows further heightened within Dan Guthry. The outlaw must be made to pay — to suffer — to understand the sanctity of life.

The meal was ready. Flood returned, filled his plate and cup, squatted, back to the cottonwood, and began to eat. Guthry crossed to the house, paused at its corner. Juan Severo had not moved.

"There is food," he called. "You are welcome to what we have."

Severo's shoulders twitched. "I have no hunger," he said, and then added with the inborn politeness of his kind, "I thank you."

Dan turned away. When he was again with Flood and had taken up his plate, he said, "Better change our sleeping place — move to the barn."

The marshal's face crinkled into a frown. The day's harsh sun had darkened his forehead considerably but an angry pink was still visible beneath his stubble of whiskers.

"Why? You think the Mexican fellow will try leaving without waiting for young Maxwell?"

"Taking no chance on it. He'll need a horse if he does. Our sleeping in the barn will stop him from getting one."

"Like I told you, could tie him up, make sure." The lawman paused, raised his head. "Nobody's going to stand in the way of the Almighty!"

Dan blinked, then sighed. Flood was back on the old track again. He wagged his head. "No need — and it wouldn't be right. Severo's had it hard enough for one day."

"Small one — Manuel," Juan Severo droned softly into the darkness, "all is not lost. I will not let it be so. The world has robbed you of your mother, of your father, and now of your own life. But I am here, little one. Be strong, young grandson so beautiful. You will not be forgotten. Rest now in the arms of your mother . . ."

"The gringos and their law will not have their way. True, no longer is the land a part of the Mother

Country of Mexico, but such means nothing. A man's heart, a people's proud way does not change because a boundary line is made. The ancient system of honor lives on and cannot be wiped away by the writing of names on paper."

It was sad. So fine a home was Manuel having. The old gentleman and his lady were treating him as a son. He was learning, being taught many fine things — the proper things of how to read and write — and such elegant manners! A credit to the family name of Severo which, long before the French came, was of great consequence. A true gentleman he would have become.

But the one with the evil eyes and hair of red color had changed all. He had brought the bright promise to an end. One man — one heartless, cruel gringo had brought to a close the young life that showed such promise.

And now other gringos would forbid him, the grandfather, to exact the vengeance that he was bound by ties of blood to take! They were nothing — these gringos! Small insects upon the face of a land that knew law and culture before their forebears even looked upon the clean sand.

Ignore them. Such was what must be done. Harm them, no. Ignore them, go his way into the Espantoso, track down the one with the evil eyes, slay him as one would the wolf that came to prey on the goats . . . He would not be alone in such. Lot Maxwell would accompany him, be at his side. Lot would think as did he, would understand his ways and know what must be accomplished.

Had not Lot been his friend since the days when he was no larger than Manuel? Had he not gone with him many times to tend the goats? Had they not eaten and slept and prayed together? Yes, Lot would again be his close companion, and the need for vengeance would fill his heart, too.

But care must be employed. The young lawman who spoke the tongue with such ease was no fool. Also he was honest from the heart and sincere in what he said. Such was evident. But the other, the red-faced one with the look of the possessed in his eyes — he was the one in whom no trust should be placed. Why would a man such as he, seemingly a holy one, be also a man of the law? The gringos had even stranger ways than he had thought.

With the coming of the sun they would ride, it had been said. Good. Let them ride, be well gone. Lot Maxwell would come and together they would also begin a journey, one that would end in great satisfaction for each. No matter if the gringo lawmen were miles ahead, he, Juan Severo, knew the Espantoso as one knows the face of his only child. He and Lot would find the red-haired man of evil first.

"Sleep, little grandson," he murmured. "All is well."

CHAPTER
NINE

Astride their horses, ready for departure, Dan Guthry and Deputy Marshal Flood looked down at the frail figure of Juan Severo in the pale, pre-dawn light. The aged Mexican seemed even smaller, his features more wizened.

"I would know," Severo said in his gentle Spanish, "how death came to my grandson. Also to the old gentleman and his lady. It will be a question asked of me by the son."

"The bullets of a pistol," Guthry replied. "Death came quickly." He did not mention the subsequent voracious attack of the vultures. It would serve no purpose.

"It matters little," Severo said. "Death is death. It is only that I wish to know all."

"You will tell the Maxwell son when he comes here of what is being done by us?"

"I shall tell."

"You will also tell him he must not interfere? That punishment of the assassin must be left to the law? This is also understood by you, Juan Severo?"

"I have heard you."

"To such you agree?"

Severo shrugged in the timeless manner of people accustomed to accepting the will of others, yet within their hearts agreeing to none of it. Dan waited, and then finally he, too, stirred. He would get no definite assurance from the Mexican, only vagueness.

"*Adios, viejo*," he said, lifting the sorrel's reins, wheeling him about.

"*Adios*," Severo replied. His omitting the customary blessing of the deity in his farewell was conspicuous.

As they moved off through the orchard toward the slumbering Espantoso, Guthry felt Flood's burning eyes drilling into him.

"What was all that palavering about?"

"Just warning him to stay put, not try running Sul Rich down. Him or Maxwell."

"What'd he say?"

"Not much, one way or the other."

There was a brief silence and then in a surprisingly harsh tone, the old lawman said: "He's not to interfere! You should have seen to that!"

"Seen to it — how? Tied him to a post? Left him to die if Lot Maxwell shouldn't show up? He hasn't committed any crime — and there're limitations to the authority of the law. You know that, Marshal, same as I do."

"Time comes when it's often necessary to take greater authority. Doing like I said so's he couldn't give us trouble would've been right!"

"Not the way I look at it."

"The way you look at it! You're only a man — a man of man's law! The Almighty's law —"

Guthry closed his ears. He was in no mood for Erland Flood's lectures on priorities, and there were more important matters to think of. He lifted his glance. The Espantoso was coming into view, barely discernible through the morning haze beyond the rim of the bench-like mesa across which they were riding.

Sul Rich, a stranger to the country, would stick to the main trail, one that followed the bottom of the vast expanse — and the line of least resistance. Thus it entailed considerably more miles than had it taken a direct route to the settlement of Ellenburg at the far end.

There were many other little known trails, difficult in places where they sliced boldly across a butte or a jutting finger of ragged lava rock, but they were seldom used and then only by those who knew them well. The danger of becoming lost far outweighed the advantage in miles and hours saved in the journey.

It was a risk he must assume, Dan Guthry decided, believing that his memory of the various secondary paths would not fail him. To trim a day off the outlaw's lead would mean much — could even bring about his early capture if luck was with them.

But he'd say nothing to Flood about it. The marshal undoubtedly would object, insist they stay on Rich's exact trail, doggedly follow him and all the while declaring that Providence, in some mysterious way, would make it possible for them to overtake the man despite the distance separating them.

That was a fool's way of looking at it. Sul Rich no longer was at a disadvantage. He had rested his horse as well as himself at the Maxwells'. He would also have provisioned fully with food and water; and he would have made inquiries, discussed thoroughly the journey he proposed to undertake with Rafe, familiarized himself with the dangers and hardships he would face.

Had he rushed blindly into the Espantoso after fleeing Lawsonville, the story would be different, perhaps would come to a conclusion that very day. But that was not the way of it; Rich was on even terms insofar as preparations for the arduous trip were concerned; his one lack was a knowledge of the land into which he dared venture. And that solitary item was the one weapon Dan Guthry knew he must make efficient use of.

With the heat rising sharply, they reached the edge of the bench late in the morning, pulled to a halt. Below them the ground fell away steeply, flowing down into a broad, sunken basin the wall of which, meeting at this end, spread quickly away, became at once distant, varicolored and rough faced.

Rugged gullies and canyons filled with jagged rock, with thornbush, greasewood and other thin growth, ran in all directions as if some powerful hand poised high above had permitted a huge drop of water to fall, splatter, run to all points, carving irregular courses in helter-skelter fashion.

Countless formations lifted themselves from the uneven floor of the sink, evidence of some primeval subterranean turbulence, shaping small, unscalable mesas, stately castle-like monoliths, and weird, wind eroded configurations that more properly fit in the dark, wild recesses of a nightmare.

To it all, under the blazing sun, there was a drab, gray sameness, a lifelessness that laid a stillness upon the two men, hushing their comments, filling them with a breathless awe and uneasiness as they looked out upon the savage grandeur. Finally Erland Flood spoke, and then but a single word.

"Purgatory."

Guthry grunted his agreement. "Fires are down there, too — the kind you can't see, only feel. Gets up to a hundred and thirty at times."

"A fitting place for the sinner. The Almighty's choice for exacting penance."

"Don't know about that," Guthry drawled. "But there's an old saying that when a man crosses the Espantoso, he doesn't go to hell when he dies. He's already been there."

Flood ignored the faint humor, his squinting eyes staring into the endless waste. "Which way we go?"

Guthry was digging into his saddlebags. After a moment he produced a pair of old army field glasses. The leather was badly worn and the brass parts shone brightly from age and much handling.

"About all we can do is head south," he said, bringing the lens into focus. "Can't see the formations that stand at the yonder end, of course, but they're called the Needle-rocks."

He picked up the trail far below, followed it painstakingly through the glasses until a bulging shoulder of rock barred his line of vision. It was devoid of any traveler. He had expected that. Rich would be much farther along and well into the heart of the Espantoso by that hour.

"Well, this ain't getting us nowheres," Flood said, his tone impatient.

Guthry hung the glasses on the horn of his saddle, touched the sorrel with his heels. The big red horse moved forward, gingerly at first, feeling his way down the steep, rock studded path. But a short time later, after the first abrupt drop off the mesa was behind him, and the trail had leveled off slightly, he began to move with more assurance.

Dan glanced over his shoulder. Flood's black was also proceeding cautiously, and the old lawman exhibiting his knowledge of horseflesh under such circumstances, was allowing the gelding to have his head. It was a welcome revelation to Dan Guthry. He was beginning to think the marshal lacked experience in many things; that he knew how to ride and handle a horse was a relief.

An hour later, with the heat a fierce, stifling enemy lashing at them with noonday fury, they reached bottom. Off to their right the skeleton of a horse lay bleaching in the sun, bones starkly white, the skull with its large eye sockets, long jaws with several broad teeth missing, seemingly a grim warning as to what lay before them.

"Who —" Flood said, pulling at his buckskin jacket, tearing at the buttons in his haste to remove it, "was that?"

"Only a wild horse — mustang," Dan replied. "Been there a long time. Fell off the bluff, I expect — with a lion after him."

There were more skeletons farther on in the burning, hostile desolation of the Espantoso. Not all were of horses.

Lot Maxwell stood silently in the noonday sun and stared at the crude markers on the three mounds of earth, already dried to powder consistency by the intense heat.

Rafe . . . Mrs. Maxwell . . . Mexican Boy . . .

Names . . . That was all his father and mother had meant to the men who had buried them. Names — and that was nothing. A name did not reflect the truth, did not tell of one man's far reaching kindness, of his gentle ways; a name could not portray the graciousness, the abiding faith and generosity of a woman who had lived . . .

A name could not recount the endless hours of back-breaking labor, of heartache, of disappointment and sacrifice. And to those who would later pass by, pause to glance, the graves would represent only names as they did to the men who had marked them.

But to a few who had come that way there would be greater meaning. They would recall that the door of the Maxwell home was always open — to the destitute, the friendless, the weary — yes, even to the outlawed. No man ever asked and was denied. So it was since he could recall; from the time when he was a small boy scurrying about in the dusty yard, playing with the homeless dogs that, like their human counterparts, drifted in to stay awhile and later move on.

Those two men could not have known any of that. Yes, it was good of them to bury, to perform the last human act, but it had been one of necessity; there had existed no feeling, no love in the transaction, merely duty.

"You are right, Uncle," Lot Maxwell murmured in Spanish to the slight figure at his elbow. "It is not enough. They are deserving of more."

Juan Severo nodded. "The old ways are best."

"You have spoken to me of the old ways. I do not always understand, but there is a voice that tells me of a service I must perform — a debt that must be paid."

"That is of the old ways."

"You are doubtless right, I cannot say. But to seek out and slay the one who has slain my parents seems right, it will not bring them back to this place they loved and for which they labored — and perhaps they will not know if vengeance is taken by me —"

"They will know."

"It is I who will know, of that I am certain. And until such is a fact there can be no rest for me. I shall hunt down this man of red hair and kill him."

"I, too, have suffered a great loss. It is my duty also."

"We are brothers in such a cause."

"Together we will find this evil one. Together we will take his life in forfeit for those of our own blood."

Lot nodded. "The trails of the Espantoso are known to you. He will follow the plain one. You can lead us by a shorter path that will enable us to overtake him?"

80

"With ease."

Again Maxwell bobbed his head. "What of the two lawmen?"

"It is likely they will also follow the trail that is plainest. Have no worry of them. By this hour they will be far ahead and will not see us when we enter the badland country. We will follow a path around them, also."

"Then it is best we start soon — after preparations are made."

"All is ready. I have selected one of your father's horses for myself. You will ride your own unless you decide otherwise."

"He will do," Lot said, and then, a faint smile on his lips, he threw his arm about the shoulders of the older man. "You knew well what would be in my heart, Uncle, and thus could read my thoughts even before I came."

Juan Severo's thin shoulders stirred. "Why is that strange? Are you not as a son to me? Are we not of the same mind and honor the same things? Come, let us go."

CHAPTER
TEN

The day was interminable, exhausting, but eventually the rim of the Espantoso lifted its ragged edge to screen the glaring ball of fire and permit the shadows to come forth, spread their welcome darkness and dull the blade of the appalling heat.

Streaks of color began to appear in the formations; reds, pale blues, ochers, and the lifeless gray of the cactus and snakeweed assumed a gentler sage green, while the scarlet tips of the ocotillos seemed to glow like small lanterns in the crimson glare of the sky.

Morose and sullen throughout the blistering day, Erland Flood said: "When we stopping? I'm about done in."

Guthry pointed wearily to a free standing formation of sandstone thrusting up from a basin of golden sand. "Camp there — on the east side. Be cooler and some protection from the wind."

"Wind," the marshal muttered. "Ain't a breath stirring."

"It'll come. Always does," Dan said laconically.

He was giving thought to the advisability of traveling at night during the cooler hours. But from times past he knew there was actually small advantage in such a plan. There were no protected places in which to hole up and rest during the day, and to simply stand and wait in the sun's scorching blast was as exhausting for both man and beast as to push on. Only at night was it possible to find relief, recover and be in condition to face a new day.

Sul Rich would not know this; he could be moving at night, seeking rest in the daylight hours. If such were true, would he not now be coming within reach? Dan Guthry couldn't answer that — and he was too beat to mull over the probability. Endeavoring to outguess the unknown was foolishness, anyway.

Tomorrow things would begin to change. The butte where he planned to make camp marked a division in the trail. To the west of the formation the main path ran on, following the flow of the land, winding in and out, snake like, with frustrating abandonment.

To the east lay a direct path that led across a long, sandstone hogback. It was rough, hard on a horse, but it avoided the many switchbacks encountered in the other, and over a length of twenty miles or so it saved at least half. Be smart to plan its use and to do so their mounts would need a full night's rest. Tomorrow accomplished, he would then think about the succeeding day.

Darkness came as they pulled up beneath the butte. Camp was simple, preparations few. Dan suggested Flood see to their meal this time while he looked after the horses. He would rest easier in mind knowing that he had cared for them personally — not that he now doubted the marshal's ability or trustworthiness to enact such a chore . . . But in the Espantoso a man on foot was a man dead.

After feeding and watering the sorrel and Flood's black, rubbing them down with one of the blankets, Guthry found he had barely enough strength left to look to his own needs. He'd forgotten how the constant, hammering heat sapped a man, sucked him dry not only of moisture but of vitality as well.

Sprawled, propped on one elbow, he ate disinterestedly of the food Flood had prepared. Only the coffee tasted good — probably because it was in liquid form.

"From here we go careful," he said, putting his plate aside. It could wait until morning for cleaning. "No fires until dark and then only a little one."

The marshal paused in his eating. "You figure we're that close to him?"

"Not him I'm thinking about. Apaches."

Flood resumed his meal. "We likely to run into a bunch of them?"

Guthry shook his head. "They don't prowl the country much. Nothing down here to hunt. But they don't like trespassers and smoke will draw them quick. Smart to take no chances."

"Can't figure out them savages. Country ain't no good, still they don't want a man riding through it. Makes no sense."

"Way an Apache thinks never does. Some figure they consider this sacred ground. Maybe it was in time past — I don't know. Could be they're just making a stand. Whites, have taken over about everything else they called their own, and they just don't aim to be pushed any farther. So they're hanging onto the Espantoso, worthless or not."

Guthry lay back flat. His arm ached. His head throbbed dully, but a faint coolness had slipped into the sink, tempering the heat, easing somewhat his discomfort. Somewhere close by a rock cracked sharply as its temperature began to lower. Far off in the distance an owl hooted. An owl or an Apache. Could be either. He reached for his blanket, spread it beneath his jaded body.

Savoring the luxury of simply stretching, easing the muscles of his legs, his back, his shoulders, he stared up into the velvet, spangled sky. Flood was snoring deeply, asleep almost as quickly as he had lain down. One of the horses shifted, blew wearily. Again the owl hooted, distant, lonely.

Unexpectedly his thoughts swung to Cathren Keel, the recollection of her standing there on the hotel's porch, arm raised in farewell, etched clearly in his mind's eye.

She was a beautiful woman in many ways — and a fine one, he'd decided the first time they had met. And she'd had no easy time with life. This he had learned during the three or four times they had encountered each other in Lawsonville's Trailrider Cafe. Each living alone and taking meals out, their meeting had been accidental and entirely natural.

Cathren had been friendly, yet reserved, but he had managed to learn that she was originally from the east; that her father, a railroad man, had been killed, after which her mother had supported her and a younger sister by dressmaking. A year or so later the mother followed the father in death and the task of earning the livelihood and raising a sister seven years her junior fell upon the still young shoulders of Cathren.

Business was considerably less than good in the town where they resided, but there was cash enough to make the move to Wichita where Cathren had heard things were booming. She found this to be true; cattlemen were prone to dressing their womenfolk well, and her shop prospered.

But misfortune struck again. Loretta, the sister, had died. Under what circumstances or for what reason Cathren did not say, but not long afterwards she had sold out, moved on west, coming finally into Lawsonville. She liked the town, she'd told Dan, was thinking seriously of opening a dress shop there . . . He hoped she would . . . It was nice being with her . . . Maybe — in the future . . .

It was the wind that aroused Guthry. He sat up, glanced to the east. A pale flare of pearl was beginning to show. Pulling himself erect, he flexed, crossed to where Flood yet slept, nudged the lawman with his toe.

The marshal came awake instantly. "What —"

"Time we got moving."

Flood grunted, scrubbed at his jaw now covered with a heavy, black stubble. Guthry squatted beside his saddle, unbuckled one of the leather pouches and fished out a quart bottle of whiskey. Pulling the cork, he offered the liquor to the lawman.

"Goes good this time of the morning."

Flood shook his head. "Poison. Destroys a man instead of helping him. Coffee'll do me fine."

Dan shrugged, took a healthy pull at the bottle and restored it to its place in his saddlebags. "Keep that fire small," he said and moved on to take care of the horses.

Giving each a little grain, he began to throw on the gear, taking care with the saddle blankets, and leaving the bridles until last. He'd give them a measure of water after they'd finished off the oats, then slip the headstalls into place.

Breakfast — bacon, hardtack soaked and fried in grease; coffee, black and strong, was ready by the time his chores were finished. The two men ate in hurried silence, cleaned and packed their equipment and were mounted and moving off by the time the round ball of the sun pushed over the rim in the east and began its climb.

The trail was worse than he had expected, but it had been years since he followed it. Erland Flood became aware of the change immediately.

"Why ain't we taking the regular way?"

"Save a lot of time on this trail."

"Maybe. Going to be slow traveling, can see that if it's like this all along. Good place for a horse to bust a leg, too. Seems smarter to stay down there on the flat."

"Got to cut Rich's lead if we can," Guthry said patiently. "He gets out of the Espantoso we could lose him quick. Mexican border's only about twenty-five miles from where we climb out."

"Thought you said there was a settlement there."

"There is — Ellenburg. Short ways back from the rim. Nothing guarantees us he'll stop there. Could keep right on going for that Mexican town on the border."

"He won't be doing that. He'll stop."

Guthry made no immediate reply. Then, as an afterthought, "You bring a letter that will let us go on into Mexico after him if we have to?"

"Letter?"

Dan Guthry frowned, glanced at the lawman. "Something from your office that we can show the Mexican officials, prove we're authorized to enter their country to capture an outlaw. Doctrine of Pursuit, I think they call it."

Flood said: "Probably among my papers."

"Probably!" Guthry exploded, swiping at the sweat on his face. "Hell, man, it'd better be! We're in big trouble if you don't have it and we're forced to go across the line." Moments later he added: "Figured that'd be about the first thing you'd see to, considering the direction we'd be heading."

"It'll be there," Flood said, his tone edgy.

"What if it's not?"

"We'll go in anyway. Man's law comes second to that of the Almighty. And I've been given the task —"

"Oh, for hell's sake!" Guthry exclaimed in disgust, and turned his attention back to the trail.

The day wore on, little different from the one that preceded. Blistering heat, blinding sun ruling a hushed world in which there appeared to be no living creatures other than two men on weary horses crawling with infinite slowness across the seared land.

And then near dark there came change.

Two more figures appeared, moving in from a point farther to the east. For a time they advanced at seemingly equal pace, and then it became clear the newcomers were pursuing a more direct route, that the two parties would converge eventually at a point where a towering finger of stone pointed accusingly at the pitiless sky.

Dan Guthry saw the riders when he and Flood topped out a low ridge, drew to a halt. Raising his glasses, he trained them on the distant men, swore softly.

"Severo," he muttered aloud. "That'll be Lot Maxwell with him. I'd hoped he'd be smart enough to stay out of this."

Flood regarded him from his pocketed eyes. "Means they're out after Jame — Rich, too."

"No other reason they'd be coming this way," Dan replied. Again he studied the approaching pair. "Took a different trail — short cut. If we'd stuck to the regular path they'd come out ahead of us before dark."

"There a chance we can keep in front of them?"

"Afraid not. Severo knows this country a lot better than me. Best thing we can do is pull up, wait for them. Expect they're figuring we're miles to the west."

"You meaning for us to join up with them?"

Dan nodded. "You think of a better way to keep tabs on them than having them with us?"

Flood shook himself angrily. "All right — but I'll stand for no trouble from them. It's my job to —"

"No, Marshal," Dan broke in sharply. "Heard you say that before. It's my job. I'm the man after Sul Rich. You're along to help, if I need any. Been a couple or three times along the way when you seemed to think it was a personal deal of yours — this catching Rich. Not that way at all. Don't forget that. He's my prisoner. I aim to catch him, take him back and see him hung."

Flood's jaw was set to a hard line. His eyes glowed fiercely from their shadowed recessions.

"Don't forget it," Guthry repeated, his gaze never wavering.

Abruptly Erland Flood nodded. Satisfied, Guthry swung his attention away to Maxwell and Juan Severo. Anger still pulsed through him and he silently cursed Henry Lawson for saddling him with a man he neither wanted nor needed. That moment of temper had been coming for some time, but now what had needed saying had been said. Perhaps things would go a bit smoother.

Again he picked up the trail the two men were following. Holding his glasses upon it, he traced its course. By moving ahead he saw where he and Flood could take up a position behind a large wedge of rocks and brush and there, unseen, await the arrival of Severo and Maxwell, and intercept them.

"Let's move out," he said crisply, offering no further explanation as he put the sorrel into motion.

Flood moved in behind him silently and they dipped down into a narrow swale studded with sprawling clumps of prickly pear cactus covered with yellow blossoms, and spurred their horses to a trot. Shortly they reached the wedge and halted. Dismounting. Dan

90

led the sorrel to the blind side of the rocks, secured him to a mesquite bush. He waited until Flood had followed a similar procedure, and then together they hurried to the lower end of the formation.

"Be passing in front of us," Dan said. "Best we take them by surprise, feeling the way they do."

Flood mopped his face and neck. "You making prisoners of them?"

"Sort of. Don't want them getting in the way."

"That Mexican fellow — don't trust him much."

"He'll bear close watch. So will Maxwell," Dan said, and thought: *not sure I can trust you either, Marshal.* He leaned up against the rocks, jerked away; the intensity of the stored heat was so great that it could blister.

"Could take their guns, send them packing," Flood suggested.

"Not in this country. Might as well just shoot them down, leave them lay. With the Apaches around most anywhere would amount to the same thing."

Guthry removed his hat, peered cautiously around the shoulder of rock. Maxwell and Severo were still a half mile distant, coming on steadily. Sunlight glinted off the weapons they carried, and from the —

The metallic click of rifle being cocked brought Dan Guthry around swiftly. He stiffened, dropped his hand to his pistol — froze. A dozen Apaches, their copper skins glistening with sweat, faced him.

CHAPTER
ELEVEN

Flood saw the change in Guthry, wheeled. His jaw snapped shut and anger burned in his eyes.

"Careful," Guthry warned softly.

The Indians, rifles lifted, closed in. One near center of the half circle, evidently a chief, barked something in the guttural tongue of his tribe, pointed toward the east. They were aware of the two men coming down the trail, planned to make prisoners of them also.

The chief, a lean, muscular man clad only in a dirty, cotton loin cloth, horsehide leggins, and with a strip of red cloth around his head, voiced another command. Two braves dropped from their ponies, hurried forward. One disarmed Flood, the second, Guthry.

Dan swore in silent frustration. He'd taken every care and precaution, and it had still worked out wrong. They were in Apache country, but encountering a war party in this particular area without doing something to attract them was a ten to one shot . . . Sul Rich . . . The explanation came to him in that next moment. Evidently the outlaw had drawn their attention, brought them in from their customary range farther west. Odds were the outlaw was dead — or at least a prisoner.

"Go!" The chief's order was a harsh, explosive sound as he pointed to their horses.

Guthry, walking slowly under the watchful, black eyes of two braves, moved toward his sorrel. A stride away Erland Flood had not stirred, held stubbornly to his ground.

"Don't give them any argument," Dan said.

The marshal swept the Apaches with a withering glance. "Heathen," he muttered, and then starting for his horse, added: "What're they aiming to do?"

"Take us back to their camp, probably. Want us out of the way right now so's they can grab Maxwell and Severo . . . Ought to yell, try and warn —"

"No talk!" the chief snapped, gesturing angrily.

Endeavoring to alert the two men would be useless, anyway, probably serve only to get himself clouted over the head. Lot and the old Mexican were too far away to hear a shout.

He swung onto the saddle. Flood was a bit slower in getting on the black. One of the braves kneed his pony in close, prodded the marshal sharply in the ribs with the muzzle of his rifle. Flood recoiled, furious. The Indians laughed.

The chief said something. Four Apaches immediately closed in on the lawmen, motioned for them to move out, head toward the center of the sink. Behind them at the rocky wedge the remainder of the party were taking positions behind the larger boulders as they shaped up their ambush.

The brave in front of Guthry veered into a deep arroyo, the east side of which was formed by a high wall of red sandstone pocked with holes and several caves of fair size. He led the party on for a quarter mile or so while the wash gradually deepened into a small canyon, and then finally drew to a halt.

At once the Apaches formed a loose circle around the two men, facing them, rifles leveled, from four sides. It was apparent they were to wait there for the rest of the braves.

Dan studied the dark, paint daubed face of the man directly before him. He was young, sat his gray pony with an easy, indolent grace. The rifle he held was an old army Springfield. A hide pouch of spare cartridges hung from one shoulder.

"Who is chief?" Guthry asked in Spanish.

The brave made no reply, continued to stare in a fixed, hating way. Dan was certain he understood the question; Apaches, as a whole, had adopted the tongue. He twisted his head, being careful not to move his body, looked at the brave to his left. He was somewhat older than the other, with a leathery leanness that came from constant riding and battling environment as well as man. Guthry repeated the question.

"Gordo," the Indian replied.

The younger Apache exploded a string of angry sounds. The man to Dan's left shrugged. In the tense hush that followed Erland Flood shifted his weight, raised a hand to wipe at the sweat accumulated on his face. Instantly the Indians came to sharp alert.

Guthry swore. "Don't do that again if you want to keep on living . . . This is a trigger happy bunch, about as jumpy as I've ever seen."

The young brave, abruptly enraged by the sound of Dan's voice, yelled something, surged forward with his rifle poised to club. Guthry ducked away as the butt of the weapon swept by, missing by inches.

The older Apache rapped several reproving words at the brave, and then facing Guthry, snarled: "*Silencio!*"

Dan Guthry settled back, again cursing the misfortune of being captured by the Apaches — and the very real probability of having lost Sul Rich. If the outlaw had managed to slip through the Indians, he would be moving farther beyond reach with every minute; if he was also a prisoner the situation was only a little better.

Either way his chances for returning Rich to Lawsonville were growing dimmer. As a lawman — his thoughts came to a halt, a stream of hope trickling through him.

Maybe there were possibilities in the fact that he and Erland Flood were lawmen in pursuit of an outlaw who must be caught and punished. Apaches understood law and punishment, practiced a system of their own. Perhaps he could make them see his position. He'd talk to the chief. But he'd have to explain carefully, be certain of what he said.

The sound of horses was suddenly upon them, and then loud words and much laughing. The remainder of the party rode down into the canyon, Juan Severo and Maxwell in their midst. Both appeared to be unharmed, had evidently been taken without a struggle.

The Indians were flushed with success . . . Three white men and a Mexican — and no shooting of bullets, the young chief was crowing as they drew near. It was a good hunt. Three rifles, one of the long guns that throws many iron pellets, two pistols and ammunition for all. It was a great find. Was not Delgazin worthy of being chief?

Delgazin . . . That was the young chief's name. But the older brave had spoken of a leader called Gordo. Likely Delgazin was only a sub-chief, and out to build a name for himself. Such wouldn't make matters easier.

"Here we camp!" Delgazin said, leaping lightly from his horse.

He held Flood's Winchester in his left hand, Dan saw. The marshal's pistol was tied to his waist by a leather string. His own weapon, the rifle anyway, was in the possession of another brave. He could not locate his revolver.

He turned to glance at Maxwell and Severo, felt a hand grip his arm, drag at him roughly. Kicking free of the stirrups, he came off the saddle. One of the braves shoved him forward, pointed at one of the larger caves in the wall of the bluff. Ahead of him Maxwell and Juan Severo were being accorded similar treatment, and shortly all three were inside the too small enclosure, standing in half bent position. A moment later Erland Flood came stumbling in.

"Savages," the old lawman muttered, catching at Severo to keep from falling.

Dan's attention moved to Lot Maxwell. He doubted if the younger man would remember him. Lot had been a small boy when last he had visited the Maxwell homestead, and then he had been there for only overnight.

"Name's Guthry," he said in a low voice. "Knew your folks. My partner's Erland Flood, a deputy U.S. marshal."

Maxwell nodded coldly. Out on the sandy floor of the small canyon the Apaches were horsing around, laughing, yelling noisily. A fire had been lit. Delgazin's voice lifted above the confusion.

"Search the packs for food."

Severo said: "These are the men of whom I spoke."

Maxwell, face taut, nodded again. "Obliged to you for seeing after ma and pa. And the boy."

"Only sorry we got there too late."

"The man who done it — any sign of him yet?"

"None. Good chance the Apaches've got him, too. Soon as things settle down a bit I aim to try talking to them. Who's Gordo?"

"Their big chief," Maxwell said. "He's not out there in that bunch. I don't know who that one is giving all the orders."

"Delgazin. Heard him say it when he was doing his bragging a few minutes ago. We'll have to deal with him unless they take us back to their main camp."

Maxwell shook his head. "You won't have much luck."

"Got to try. I'll try to make them understand that we're lawmen, after a killer who —" Guthry paused as a new idea came to him. The Apaches had never bothered Rafe Maxwell, even during times when Indian trouble was widespread. "— who murdered the

Maxwells, friends of the Apache. I'll stretch it a bit, say the killer tried to make it look like the Apaches did it."

Lot considered that, his gaze on the milling braves. They had dug into the sack that Juan Severo had tied to his saddle, were pawing through the provisions it contained.

"Won't work," he said. "Pa got along with them mostly because he was that way — could get along with anybody. But that was with Gordo and the older bucks. This young bunch ain't going to see things in the same light as they did."

Guthry shrugged. "Saw a couple of old heads in the bunch . . . I'm looking for suggestions. You think of anything better?"

"Way I see it, not much we can do — set and wait."

Dan stared at Lot, surprised to hear such resignation from a man so young. He would expect it from Severo, and then he remembered Rafe Maxwell had more or less been of the same turn; simply hold back, accept things as they came and hope for the best. *Not for me*, Guthry thought, and turned to Juan Severo.

"Old one, if it is possible to talk with this Delgazin, it must be in the language of your people. He must understand clearly. There are words I have forgotten and I fear to say things that are wrong. I will need to speak through you."

The Mexican's dark face squeezed into a frown. "We are all enemies of the Apache, but they have a greater hatred for my race. I fear it would be unwise —"

"To talk is our one hope," Guthry said impatiently. "This you must know. Our lives could be saved by you."

Severo lowered his head. "Agreed. When you are ready I shall speak."

CHAPTER
TWELVE

The moment was not long in coming.

The Apaches, after ransacking Severo's supplies, had turned to Guthry's sorrel. They discovered first of all the bottle of whiskey he carried, and promptly all thoughts of food were forgotten. Yells went up and the braves gathered in a tight cluster near the fire where the bottle quickly made the rounds. At once the mood of the party began to change as the liquor took effect.

Delgazin stood in the center of the group, rifle held aloft, face turned to the darkening sky. Firelight danced upon his glistening body, glinted off the weapon in his hand. Suddenly he raised his other arm, and opening his mouth, gave voice to a shrill cry that echoed along the wash.

Other braves took it up, began to dance, hopping on one foot and then the other while they kept the closing night alive with their yells. Two broke from the knot, wrestling for possession of the near empty bottle. The smaller of the pair succeeded, darted off to one side. Tipping the bottle, he drained it of its last drop, and then with a guttural oath of some sort, dashed it against the face of the canyon wall.

The container shattered, the glass dropping a few paces below the cave where the prisoners were quartered.

"Wish now there'd been two quarts, instead of one," Guthry murmured.

"Plenty there to get them drunk," Lot said. "Not used to whiskey."

Dan wasn't so sure. They could have gotten just enough to make them mean, difficult to deal with. Another quart to pass around and they likely would have dropped in their tracks.

"They come," Severo said softly, and crossed himself.

Guthry glanced up. A half dozen laughing, shouting braves swaggered up to the cave. One reached in, seized Maxwell by the arm, jerked him into the open. The others made signs for the rest to follow. Pushed, shoved, slapped at, the four men were herded into the center of a circle beyond the fire.

At once Delgazin leaped to his feet. "Chief — me, Delgazin!" he yelled, thumping his chest. He seemed less affected by the whiskey than some of his followers.

One of the older men said, "Hah!" and spat in disgust.

Delgazin pounded again on his expanded chest. "Chief!" he declared once more.

Guthry glanced at his companions, nodded, took a step forward. He raised his arm, hand extended palm outward.

"You are Delgazin, chief," he said in Spanish. "Are you the great chief? The leader of all the Apaches?"

Delgazin paused, appeared startled to hear words of Spanish coming from a white man. He abandoned his broken English.

"I am the strongest of all!"

Again the old brave displayed his disapproval.

"Who is Gordo?"

Delgazin frowned darkly, spat, slapped at his haunch to express his derision. "An old one not with strength and wisdom to lead the people."

"It is you who takes his place?"

The Apache bobbed his head violently. "I am chief."

"Then it is to you I will speak."

Delgazin's shoulders came back proudly. "Of what can a prisoner talk to one who is his captor?"

Guthry's gaze swept the circle. Two of the braves were dozing, the liquor having had its way. Those remaining showed a keen interest in what was taking place, however. He turned, laid a hand on Juan Severo's thin shoulder.

"This old one speaks the tongue better than I," he said, again facing the young sub-chief. "I will have him put in proper words what must be said."

Delgazin spat loudly. "A Mexican! You will speak for yourself. His kind is not to be trusted."

Dan started to protest, thought better of it. Nothing could be gained by further antagonizing the Apache. He lowered his head.

"It will be as you wish. Listen well, Chief of the Apaches. My words are of great importance."

Delgazin cracked his palms together sharply. "Hear him! The rabbit that is about to be skinned will speak strong words to the wolf!"

A roar of laughter went up, accompanied by a great deal of rib poking and light horseplay. Guthry stood in rigid silence, waited for things to quiet down. When the racket had ceased, he continued.

"We are men of the law," he said, lifting the flap of his shirt pocket to show his star. "We do not mean to trespass in the land of the Apache but must do so. We search for an assassin who rode this way. Is he a prisoner in your camp?"

Delgazin frowned and a rumble of conversation made the rounds of the seated Apaches.

"Do you say there is another white man?"

Evidently Sul Rich had not fallen into the hands of this bunch. Guthry nodded.

"One who has done much evil. He has slain the friends of the Apache — Maxwell and his woman. It is also true that he tries to blame this bad thing on your people."

The young chief's eyes sparked. Another burst of talk ran through the group, some of it being in the Apache tongue.

"We have come for this assassin. We will punish him with death for his deeds. You must not stop us from doing this. Such is for the good of the Apache people as for the good of the white men."

Delgazin made an angry gesture with his hand. "The Apache does not need the law of the white man. The Apache will find this evil one and punish him well."

He was being tripped up in his own snare, Dan realized, but he could do nothing but attempt to work his way out.

"This you cannot do," he said, taking a firm stand. "The white people do not interfere with the law of the Apaches. Therefore, the Apaches must not interfere with that of the whites."

"Only Apache law has strength in the land of the Apache," Delgazin countered.

The young chief was no fool even if his tongue was getting a bit thick, his words somewhat slurred. But the firmness had scored.

"It will be wise to free us, let us search for this one who kills needlessly," Guthry pressed. "He can do much harm to your people."

"Only one white man?" Delgazin scoffed. "He will be quickly found, and then will die slowly. This is the land of the Apache where no one lives unless the Apache wills it so."

"It is your land. I agree to this. But it is in the nature of important things that we are here. We mean no harm to your people. We do not intend to remain. We only trail a man who must be made prisoner. This is all we ask of the Apache."

"No!" Delgazin yelled, and made a chopping motion with his hand. "It is finished. I talk no more."

Guthry reached for his last card. "It is not finished. I will speak with Gordo. He is a man of wisdom."

The Apache's eyes blazed with anger. His head came forward aggressively. "I am chief!"

"You are sub-chief," Guthry said, careful to show no alarm. "It is the law of your people that only the big chief can speak the will of the tribe. Thus words must be said by Gordo."

Talk was running the circle again. The older brave that Dan had spoken with earlier stared at Delgazin, a sly look on his weathered face. After a moment he said something in his native tongue. One of the others nodded. Two more took it up, all apparently agreeing on something.

Erland Flood's voice was low. "What're they saying?"

"Talking Apache. I don't know."

"Something about Gordo," Lot Maxwell said. "I think they're saying you're right, that it's up to Gordo and not Delgazin."

Guthry glanced to Lot. "You savvy Apache?"

"Only a few words. Was an old squaw lived at the place for a spell. They'd left her to die, folks took her in, looked after her."

Conversation around the circle dwindled, died. Delgazin still stood tall and proud in the glow of the leaping flames, his superb body highlighted by color and shadow. He was fighting hard to save face, Dan saw, and immediately struck another tack.

"All know Delgazin is a great chief, a brave man. He is known to be wise enough to seek the counsel of the elders in so important a matter. Such would prove to all braves that he is deserving of being chief."

105

The shot drove home. Delgazin raised his hand, glared at his warriors. "It shall be so. With the morning sun we will take the prisoners to the camp beyond the ridge, let them speak with Gordo. It is wise to hear the words of the old ones at such times. This I have decided." Again he made the chopping motion with his hand. "It is finished."

Dan Guthry breathed deeper. Several of the braves were nodding approval . . . Three more were asleep, he noted. Now, if their luck would continue to hold . . .

"Go!" Delgazin said, this time in English, and pointed at the cave.

Two of the braves pulled themselves erect, one yawning noisily, and escorted them none too gently back to the hole in the butte. Inside, Flood turned to Guthry.

"What good's us going to their camp —"

"Wait," Dan said, shaking his head.

"What for? Seems to me chances for getting away are better —"

Guthry clapped his hand over the old lawman's lips, silencing him, and pointed to the two Apaches standing just outside the opening. The braves continued to remain there as if listening, and then both moved off, shambled back to the fire.

Immediately Guthry dropped to his knees, made his way to the entrance of the cave. There, stretched out full length, he gathered in the larger pieces of the shattered whiskey bottle and hastily withdrew.

Over at the fire there was a quick explosion of angry words. Shortly one of the younger braves returned, sat down on a ledge facing the cave. Apparently Delgazin had delegated him to sentry duty.

Keeping well in the darkness of the sandstone pocket, Dan passed out the larger pieces of glass to the three men, reserving one for himself.

"Only thing we've got that'll do as a weapon," he said in a whisper.

Maxwell pointed to the guard. "Never get close enough to him. He'll shoot the minute we show our heads."

"Know that — but I'm depending on that whiskey, hoping it puts him to sleep."

"Better be pretty quick," Flood said. "It works, we'd best be a long ways from here by sunrise."

CHAPTER
THIRTEEN

The fire dwindled, became only a single tongue of darting flame. One of the Apaches stirred, reached for a handful of branches, tossed them onto the smoldering pile. The glow took heart, brightened, extended its flare.

Guthry peered at the sentry. He was dozing — but at least one of the braves sprawled around the campfire had not been asleep. There could be others. Grim, feeling the press of passing time, he continued to wait.

The minutes dragged by, became an hour. Flood began to snore softly . . . Strange man, the marshal. You'd think he'd be fully awake, anxiously looking for the moment to escape, a way to help . . . Age, perhaps, Dan thought. It could be that Erland Flood was too old for his job. That could account, too, for some of his odd ways and the peculiar things he said . . . Somewhere in the far distance beyond the rim a coyote barked into the moon-flooded night.

Something disturbed the horses, caused one to shy, rattle the brush. Instantly a brave was on his feet and cat-footing it across the circle of light created by the fire toward the mesquite clumps where the animals were tethered . . . Delgazin . . . He moved silently, like a

w. . He reached the horses, halted in the shadows. For a time he stood there, and then deciding all was well, turned back.

Midway he altered course, angled for the dozing sentry in front of the cave. The young Apache's head had dropped forward. Delgazin stared at him briefly, drew back his foot and delivered a sound kick into the brave's ribs.

A yell blurted from the younger man's lips. He sprang to his feet, rifle ready in his hands. He saw Delgazin standing before him, recoiled, looked down in shame as a torrent of words poured from the chief's mouth. After a minute or so the brave nodded, resumed his place on the ledge. Delgazin swung his eyes to the cave.

"Be asleep," Guthry murmured, tipping his face down.

The Apache drew nearer, squatted to look into the cramped cubicle. The outlines of the four prisoners would be visible to him, thanks to the moon, and the sound of Flood's snoring plain. Grunting in satisfaction, he straightened, moved back to the fire. Pausing to throw more fuel into the flames, he stretched, yawned, and once again sprawled on the warm sand.

Guthry placed his attention on the sentry. The brave was thoroughly awake now, his features clear in the half light.

"He will sleep again," Severo murmured in a confident voice.

"When he does we best make our move," Dan replied.

"Time's running out."

Delgazin was his primary worry. The young chief appeared to be having trouble dozing off. Dan glanced at the Apache's prone figure. He seemed quiet enough now.

"How we doing this?" Maxwell asked.

"You and me — we'll take care of the guard. Got to shut him up quick — before he can yell, rouse the others. Juan, while we're doing that you and the marshal slip out, get our horses. Lead them down the arroyo a piece. Not far. Don't want to have to make a long run for them. Once we're mounted, head south."

"What about guns?" Maxwell asked.

Guthry pointed to the sleeping Apaches. Each had his weapon with him, either clutched in a hand or lying close to his body.

"Try taking one and you'll have the whole bunch up on their feet . . . Won't need them anyway if we can get clear of the camp without rousing anybody."

"Reckon we'll have one rifle," Lot said. "The guard's."

Guthry said: "Don't get in a hurry to grab it and miss with that piece of glass. Killing him quick is what's going to count." He turned to Severo. "You can do this, take the horses without disturbing the Indians?"

"It is possible. With care I —"

"Unless it is done all that Lot and I do will be for nothing — and we will all surely die."

"Have no fear. The horses will be waiting."

The sentry's head bobbed forward, came up quickly, held, began to again sink slowly. Guthry reached for

Flood, shook him gently. The lawman came up with a start. Dan cursed softly, pressed his hand against the marshal's lips to stifle any further sound, and glanced at the guard. He had not been aroused. Hurriedly, he outlined the plan.

Flood nodded, said, "When?"

Dan took a final look toward the men around the fire. "Now," he said. "Wait until we get to the sentry, then move out . . . Stay low."

Nudging Maxwell, Guthry grasped the jagged piece of glass he'd salvaged, edged toward the mouth of the cave. The paradoxical aspect of the situation struck him at that moment. He and Erland Flood were working hand in glove with the two men who were out to defeat them — get to Sul Rich first and kill him — a man they were duty sworn to keep alive.

In a sense they were actually assisting Lot and Juan Severo to accomplish such, and if he and Flood did not survive the escape, and they did, a clear road would lie ahead of them . . . But it was no time for considering the odd twists of fate; they were all prisoners of the Apaches, and likely none of them would live to see another sunset if they remained in the camp until daylight.

"Ready?" he asked quietly.

Maxwell murmured in the darkness. Guthry lowered himself onto his belly, and flat, worked himself through the entrance to the cave into the open. The sentry was snoring now, fully asleep. All was quiet around the fire.

Pulling himself out onto the floor of the arroyo with care, Dan waited until Lot Maxwell had drawn abreast, and then together they wormed their way toward the Apache. Sand deadened the sound of their movements, made for easy crawling ... They reached the ledge, paused.

Behind them Severo and Flood were moving off, angling toward the horses a dozen strides below the camp. Guthry held back until the two men had disappeared into the mesquite thicket, and then touching Maxwell on the arm, nodded.

Together they rose to their knees. Each struck silently and swiftly with his dagger of glass. The brave grunted, sagged to one side. Instantly Lot Maxwell caught up the rifle from the Apache's faltering hands. Reaching across, he ripped free the pouch of cartridges that hung from the man's shoulder.

Guthry's jaw tightened. He had hoped to gain possession of the weapon for obvious reasons, but as luck would have it the rifle had fallen toward Lot. Maxwell and Severo now held the advantage insofar as the search for Sul Rich was concerned ... But they were a long way from continuing that.

Spinning about, Guthry crawled past the dead Apache, caught up with Maxwell already moving off. They gained the fringe of brush, rose to their feet, hurried on. Directly ahead they could see the dim outlines of Flood and Severo, already in their saddles, waiting with the other horses. A taut smile on his lips, Guthry reached the sorrel, vaulted aboard ... They'd made it —

A yell sounded back in the Apache camp, cut short his feeling of victory. He flung a glance up the canyon.

Beyond the screen of mesquite figures were darting about in the firelight.

"Get the hell out of here!" he rasped hoarsely, and jammed his spurs into the sorrel's flanks.

In a tight group they raced down the sandy wash. A gunshot echoed through the night, apparently one triggered by accident as none of the Indians could have seen them. But they knew the direction their escaping prisoners had taken. They were mounting up, beginning to give chase.

Dan Guthry looked ahead. The arroyo wound on, veering to their left. Immediately he swung the big gelding hard right, spurred him up the low, west embankment and through a tangle of greasewood into a flat beyond which lay a line of sandy knolls.

The move did not fool the Apaches. They had been nearer than he thought, close enough to see them when they broke out of the wash. A fresh burst of yelling lifted, and several gunshots cracked through the half dark.

Maxwell twisted about, returned the fire, but the weapon was another of the old Springfield single shot breech loaders, and its lone bullet likely went unnoticed by the oncoming braves.

They reached the low hills, dipped into a narrow ravine, the horses laboring in the sand. Guthry looked about hurriedly, tried to recall the area — failed. Nothing seemed familiar. To continue on west was wrong, anyway; ultimate escape lay to the south. At once he swerved into that direction.

113

More gunshots flatted through the night. Bullets whistled close by, thunked into the slopes of the bubble-like hillocks. Another arroyo, much narrower than the one in which the Apaches had made camp, stretched out before them, and for a short time he allowed the sorrel to pound along its road-like course, lead the way for the others.

He realized suddenly that it was a dangerous move; that in seeking easier traveling for the horses, he was placing them all in full view of the pursuing Apaches, offering them direct in-line targets. Again he cut right, forsook the wash and rushed on into the shadowy hills and low bluffs.

The horses wouldn't be able to maintain the pace much longer. The animal Juan Severo rode, accustomed to work on the Maxwell homestead, was already having difficulty in keeping up. Unless something was done quickly to throw the braves off their trail, their escape was doomed to failure.

In the distance he saw the slightly higher line of a hogback, slanting off from the formation toward which they were racing. Immediately he turned to the rider nearest him. It was Erland Flood. He yelled to draw the lawman's attention, then pointed to the dark faced bluff.

"We get there — you and the others keep to the left!"

The marshal bobbed his head, shouted: "You?"

"Aim to cut up over that ridge, draw them off."

Flood again nodded. He looked over his shoulder. The Apaches were no more than three hundred yards away, hunched, dark shapes flowing through the starshine.

"Pretty close . . . Think it'll work?"

"It'd better," Guthry said grimly. "Keep going south. I'll follow soon as I shake them. Wait for me at the Arch. Severo'll know where that is."

The deeply shadowed bluffs loomed dead ahead. Flood split away, motioning to Maxwell and Juan Severo to follow. The heaving sorrel drove straight on, labored up the short slope to the crest of the ridge.

Slowing, Guthry continued a short distance, allowed himself to be silhouetted above the rim. Bullets began to thud into the sand below him, clip through the brush. He grinned tautly. The Apaches had seen him. The trick had worked . . . Now all he had to do was save his own skin.

CHAPTER
FOURTEEN

He rode off the hogback, pointing direct west. This area was vaguely familiar — all deep sided arroyos, low buttes and round topped sandhills covered with scorched grass and snakeweed. A large canyon lay ahead, he thought, but he could not be sure. In the pale, silver light all things assumed a different, ghost-like context. He could be above the canyon — or below.

There was no yelling behind him now, only the steady drum of running horses. Delgazin and his braves had taken the bait and he had no worries as to Flood and the others. By that moment they would be well in the clear.

As for himself . . . He strained to see what lay ahead while the big sorrel thundered on through the night, dipping now into a shallow wash, racing across its sandy width, lunging up an embankment to hammer across a flat. The horse had tremendous strength but he couldn't keep up such headlong pace indefinitely.

A dark band slowly materialized in the distance. Dan peered into the night, endeavored to make out the break. The canyon? He smiled grimly. If it was — and he could reach it — his chances for throwing the

Apaches off his heels were better than good. If not —
well, it would be up to Deputy Marshal Erland Flood
to complete the task of running down Sul Rich and
taking him back to Lawsonville.

Guns rattled through the half dark, the reports sharp,
uncomfortably near. Careless, he had exposed himself
briefly as he topped the crest of another of the
countless ridges that laced the land, presented the
Apaches with a silhouetted target.

Bullets dug into the sand close by, forced him to
realize that Delgazin and his braves had narrowed his
lead dangerously. The sorrel, strong as he might be, was
no match for the wiry little Indian ponies accustomed
to racing tirelessly through the hills hour after hour.

It was not the canyon.

A tightness gripped Dan Guthry when he saw what
he thought was the hedge of brush that grew along the
rim of the slash was instead a low bench running at
right angles to the course he was following, and
extending in both directions.

The sorrel rushed toward the ledge, slowed, awaiting
his rider's decision. Guthry gave it hurried consideration,
saw there was no possibility of the horse gaining the top
because of its height, and swung left. The Apaches were
yelling now. They'd known of the bench, figured they
had their prisoners trapped against it.

Desperate, he spurred the flagging sorrel on, eyes
searching for a break in the vertical face of the ledge
that would permit him to veer off, gain the opposite
side where he might find hiding before the Apaches
closed in upon him.

It was somewhat easier going for the sorrel, and he was grateful for that. The ground along the base of the bench was firm, bedded with gravel and there was little loose sand to drag at the gelding's hooves. The big horse, it seemed, had actually increased his speed, calling up from somewhere deep in his powerful body an untapped reservoir of strength. The bench fled by, began to drop away on a long slope.

He was entering a wide, deep swale. Dark clumps marked the presence of scattered cedars; short bands of brush threw shadows upon the faintly glittering sand. But there was little substantial cover of a size to offer concealment for him and the sorrel . . . One of the larger brush clumps — he'd have to take his chances —

Guthry came up straight on the saddle. An opening in the bench had appeared — a wash, sliced into the face of the ledge by some fierce, driving rainstorm in times past, further cut by the howling winds. Relieved, he swung the sorrel into the breech, spurred him to the crest.

There was only a slight fall on the opposite side. The entire country appeared at quick glance to be a wide tableland running up to a definite rim, and there in butte formation overlooking the sink through which he had just come.

Guthry wheeled the red back onto a parallel course, doubling north. Thirty yards to his right, and below the crest, Delgazin and his followers were pressing their pursuit in the opposite direction as they followed his trail so that in effect, they passed each other with only the high bench in between.

That would not be the case for long. The Apaches would reach the break in the ledge, hesitate briefly to look for and locate the hoofprints left by the sorrel as he dug for the top, and thus assured, resume the chase.

The advantage, however, was his. Urging the gelding to his best, Dan followed the slope for a good quarter mile, and then, on the yonder side of a distinct roll of land, cut sharp right, headed for the rim of the bench. Halting in the heavy sand, he looked down. It was a long eight foot drop — a dangerous undertaking for a weary horse . . . But it was his only hope.

Pulling back a dozen paces, aware of the hammering hooves coming swiftly toward him from beyond the roll, Guthry spurred the red forward. They reached the edge of the bench, sailed off into space.

The sorrel struck solidly, went to his knees, staggered up, and plunged on into a waist high stand of weeds as momentum carried him forward. There he halted, sides heaving, head down as he sucked for wind.

Guthry dropped from the saddle, pain reawakened by the jarring impact, stabbing at his arm, throbbing inside his head. Ignoring both, he took up the reins, led the horse to a point fifty paces or so farther above and there picketed him behind a scrub cedar. Leaving his hat hanging on the saddle horn, he moved back to the bench, climbed to its level. He had thrown the Apaches off his heels — but only temporarily; he must make certain they did not turn back to the deeper part of the sink and continue their search.

Flat on his belly in the stubby, brittle growth, he looked to the slope. Sweat clothed him completely, misted his eyes. He brushed the moisture away, strained to locate the riders.

Minutes later he saw them. They had pulled their horses down to a walk, were advancing in a widely spread skirmish line. Evidently they expected him to be hiding behind one of the few brush clumps or small cedars, and were set to bring him down when flushed.

They would not be certain he had actually come that way. In Delgazin's mind would be the question whether he had doubled to the north, had instead swung to the opposite direction, or possibly fled on to the west. Only by returning to the wash and ferreting out the sorrel's hoofprints could he be absolutely sure.

But Delgazin was a proud man and apparently he wasn't ready yet to admit he could have guessed wrong on the route taken by his escaping prisoners, and return to the wash although a considerable portion of the slope had been covered.

"They are not here!"

The voice came from down grade where brush was thickest. The ragged line of horsemen pulled to a stop, little more than two dozen yards below where Guthry lay. Another of the Apaches spoke, this time in the tongue of his people, and the meaning of his guttural comment was lost to Dan.

Just which of the men was Delgazin he could not determine at that distance and in the weak light. Likely the one in the center. Abruptly the braves resumed their forward push. Somehow they were convinced he was somewhere on the slope. Alarm stirred him. He could be caught in a bad position . . . If one of the

Apaches swung wide, rode along the rim of the bench . . . He hadn't expected them to come that close.

It was too late to pull back, slip over the edge of the bench. In the night's hush the unavoidable sounds created by the scraping of clothing across the dry, stiff weeds as he crawled undoubtedly would be heard. Best he stay put, hug the ground . . .

The Apaches drew nearer, approached with aggravating, nerve-wracking slowness. It was Delgazin in the center of the line, he saw, and slightly to the front. Like the others he was bent forward, eyes probing the shadowy ground before him, rifle ready in his hands while he guided his pony with his knees.

They were abreast. Guthry breathed easier. The Indian at the near end of the line had shown no inclination to veer wide, take up a path along the rim of the bench. But he was uncomfortably close — so close Dan could hear the faint metallic click of his cartridge belt, slung bandoleer style across his shoulder, as it came in contact with his rifle.

The riders passed by, silent, intent silhouettes moving ghostlike across a tortured land turned soft and beautiful by starlight. Ten yards . . . Twenty . . . Delgazin raised an arm, shouted a command. The line halted. The Apache nearest the ledge wheeled to face his chief.

"We are wrong," he called in Spanish. "They have run to the south."

"Or to the west," another brave suggested. "There are many places where hiding can be found to the west."

121

"Would it not be wise to return to the small arroyo and find the sign of the horses?" a third voice offered.

Delgazin seemed indecisive. He cut his pony around, stared out across the route they had covered, looked then to the east. His glance, it seemed to Dan Guthry, was directly upon him.

"To the west," he said, finally. "This is also my thought. It will be wise, however, to look again onto the land below the rim."

"How can they be there? This we know is not possible since we drove them before us."

Delgazin was again staring toward the hills to the west. If they followed his idea, moved to the rim, he stood no chance of escape, Guthry realized with a tightening in his throat. Raking his mind anxiously, he sought for a way out.

He moved his arm slightly. His fingers touched the still warm, smooth shape of a stone no larger than a coffee cup. Hope surged through him as he took it into his hand.

Watching closely to be certain none of the Apaches were turned and looking in his direction, but still gazed off to the west as did their chief, he pushed himself upward. Then, employing that oldest of man's evasive tactics, he hurled the stone as far as strength permitted onto the slope beyond the riders.

The rock struck, clattered hollowly in the still night. A yell went up from the Apache at the far end of the line. Delgazin ripped out a command, and suddenly the entire party was wheeling off, racing down grade.

122

Quickly Dan Guthry pivoted, and belly-flat, worked his way to the rim of the bench. Dropping lightly to the ground below, he trotted to the waiting sorrel. He could figure on the Apaches spending at least an hour searching out the lower slope. That should give him ample time to get out of the area.

CHAPTER
FIFTEEN

Guthry held the sorrel to a walk, denying the urge to flee that part of the sink with all speed. He knew he must move quietly; in the hush the pound of hooves would carry far, could be heard by Delgazin and the others, draw them back to his trail. There could be more Apaches, also, different parties.

Too, the sorrel was near exhaustion. He'd had little rest since morning and there were still many miles to cover before they reached safety.

Two hours later he reached the line of bluffs where the party had split and he had swung west to lead Delgazin and his braves into a different part of the Espantoso. He pulled up there, gave the red gelding a brief rest, and moved on, this time heading due south.

If Flood and the two men with him had followed instructions and not become sidetracked by other Apaches, they would be waiting at the Arch, a towering rock formation in which winds had carved a natural gate through which the trail passed. With luck, he'd find them there.

Lot Maxwell was armed . . .

The full impact of the disturbing fact drilled into Dan Guthry's consciousness now that the danger from

Delgazin was gone and he had time to think. Such would make him difficult to cope with insofar as the search for Sul Rich was concerned. While neither Lot nor Juan Severo had made clear their purpose for being in the Espantoso, their determination to overtake and kill Sul Rich before the law could get to him was a foregone conclusion.

Both had ignored his warning to stay out of the affair, and further talking to Maxwell in the hope of making him see that he was in the wrong would likely prove useless. With the old Springfield in his possession he had the upper hand — and would use it . . . He'd have no better luck persuading Juan Severo, either. The old Mexican was actually more fiercely vindictive in his quiet, sullen way than Lot Maxwell.

But he must try to make them both see reason, he realized as the sorrel plodded wearily on through the silver tinted night. There was the possibility that Erland Flood had recognized the seriousness of the situation with which they were faced, had already taken steps to regain control. He hoped so, but he had doubts; somehow, as time and miles had worn on since the start of the search, his estimate of the government lawman had slipped steadily.

Guthry wasn't sure why. It was impossible to put his finger on the exact reasons, but there was something; a gnawing uneasiness that disturbed him. He'd thought of it earlier, shrugged it off, dismissed it as a dislike brought about possibly by the fact he'd been forced to work with the lawman when he preferred to handle the situation alone.

125

All of which was inconsequential. Important thing was to overtake and put the chains on Sul Rich, return him to Lawsonville . . . Anger stirred through him once again as he relived those last moments in the coulee and the personal, degrading insult he had experienced at the whim of the outlaw.

Rich would be returned to hang all right — Lot Maxwell, Juan Severo and anyone else who got in the way notwithstanding — but he would have his moment with the outlaw. Somewhere between the point of capture and the Lawsonville jail he'd take time — and pleasure — in making the outlaw crawl, eat dirt, know ignominy.

He came to a halt. Ahead the darkly outlined shape of the Arch was etched against the star splattered sky. Swinging the sorrel off the trail into a pocket of rocks, he again stopped. Just in case there'd been other Apaches, he'd best be careful, not blunder into a trap.

The night was quiet. Clucking softly to the red gelding, he moved closer, slowed as the dim shapes of horses off to his left drew attention. He counted them with difficulty . . . Three . . .

"Come on in," Lot Maxwell's voice drawled from the shadows.

Temper shortened by weariness and his close brush with Delgazin and his braves flared through Guthry. Maxwell could have called out sooner, not left him waiting out there in the darkness, wondering. Sharp words sprang to his lips, and then he shrugged, let it pass. Guiding the sorrel to where the other animals stood, he swung down, hung there for a time one hand gripping the horn, weight against the gelding's sweaty flanks while fatigue rode roughshod through him.

"You been hurt?"

It was Erland Flood. Dan shook his head, began to pull gear from the sorrel.

"The Apaches — where are they now?" Juan Severo asked in his soft, polite way.

"West of the bluffs," Guthry replied, anchoring the sorrel's neck rope. "They will not come again for us."

Digging out his rag, he watered the gelding, affixed the nose bag with a generous measure of grain. That done, he turned to the small cove in the rocks where camp had been made. No fire had been built, he saw, and was thankful the men had taken that precaution; he was in no condition for further frantic flight that night.

Lot Maxwell sat on a ledge a short distance apart, the Springfield across his knees. He straightened slightly.

"Reckon I ought to say I'm obliged to you for pulling them Apaches off our backs," he said in a grudging voice.

Dan leaned against a shoulder of stone, studied Maxwell thoughtfully. Behind him Flood and Severo were chiming in with their thanks . . . As well get to the problem of the rifle at once since it appeared Flood had made no headway if, indeed, he had even made an effort. And Lot's words did provide an opening.

"You can prove that by giving me the rifle."

Maxwell's features hardened and his jaw settled into a stubborn line. Severo crossed silently, took up a

127

position near the younger man. Flood, slumped upon a ledge at the entrance to the cove, hawked, spat.

"Been talking to him about doing that. Told him wasn't right for him to stand in the way of the law. Said he was looking out for his own law."

"Puts you in the same class with Sul Rich, Lot," Dan said with a heavy sigh. He was too beat to do much arguing about anything — and he was hungry.

"Nothing nobody could ever do would put a man that low," Maxwell replied. "Wasting your time jawing at me. I'm keeping this gun. Use it on you, too, if I have to."

"You'd shoot a lawman?" Flood asked in a rising tone.

"If one gets in the way. That killer belongs to me — and Juan. Time we're through butchering him he'll wish he'd never been born."

"Apache style, that is?" Guthry said. "Seems you maybe learned something besides a few words from them."

"You saying that killer ain't got it coming to him?"

"He's got it all coming to him — only it's up to the law to dish it out, not you. If you —"

"You can't stand in the way of justice!" Erland Flood boomed out suddenly. "You can't defy the Almighty —"

"Forget it!" Guthry snapped, fearing the sound of the old marshal's voice might carry to Apache ears as well as having no stomach for a tedious tirade on the priority of the Almighty where Sul Rich was concerned. "There anything to eat?"

128

Severo rose, moved to where the saddles were piled. Maxwell's eyes never shifted from Guthry.

"I'm keeping the gun," he said.

Guthry made no reply. Severo returned, bringing a handful of jerky, two hard biscuits and a canteen of water.

"There is little remaining. The Indians took almost all."

"Enough," Dan said. "Thank you."

"For nothing," Severo said, and returned to his place near Lot Maxwell.

He was too tired to eat. Guthry chewed at the stringy beef for a short while, gnawed at one of the biscuits, washed the tasteless bits down with a few gulps of water, then gave up. Stuffing what was left of the food into his pocket, he rose, went back to the sorrel.

The gelding had finished off the grain, anxiously hoped for an additional helping. Guthry removed the nose bag, squeezed a ration of water into the animal's mouth, and turned away. The horse deserved more of both, but they were running short — short of everything: food, water and time.

Coming back into the cove Guthry sought a comfortable spot, settled down to catch what sleep he could. They would need to leave early. Assuming Sul Rich had not been made prisoner by other Apaches, he would be far ahead by that hour.

He glanced at Maxwell, perched above the pocket on a ledge. Severo, seemingly guarding the younger man's position from approach, was slightly below. Erland Flood was dozing, shoulders against a slanting rock.

"Watch that trail," Guthry said. "Other Indians around here besides Delgazin and his bunch. I'd offer to spell you but I figure I'd be talking for nothing."

"You'd be right, Sheriff. Me and Juan — we'll do the watching. You and your friend there go ahead and get some sleep."

CHAPTER
SIXTEEN

Long before daylight they were up, mounted and moving southward through the vast Espantoso. At Lot Maxwell's stubborn insistence, Dan Guthry led off, followed by Flood and then Juan Severo, while he brought up the rear of the short column. His reasoning was clear; Lot was permitting neither of the lawmen to get behind him and make an attempt to gain possession of the party's solitary weapon.

Guthry accepted the arrangement with little comment. Lot had closed his ears to all reasoning. Best they continue without incident, put the Espantoso and the threat of Apaches behind them. When they reached Ellenburg, or drew near, then would come the time to take drastic action.

He wondered about Sul Rich as they wound their way through the early morning flare of light. Would he still be in the settlement? It seemed reasonable to think so. Figuring he had made it through the hell of the Espantoso, had managed to escape the Apaches, he would be in poor condition to travel and in bad need of rest. They were not too far behind him, making use of more direct trails; a couple of days at most.

It all depended, of course, upon how anxious the outlaw was to seek safety in Mexico, if that was what he had in mind. The comforts of the town at the end of the Espantoso would offer a powerful inducement to remain, however.

Guthry glanced to the east. Long fingers of yellow and orange were reaching upward, spraying into the gray sky. The wind had come, had its blustery way, and gone, and now the world about them was awakening. Small blue striped lizards were stirring, searching frantically for food before the sun appeared and its harsh blast forced them again to seek shade and lie dormant during the paralyzing hours of daylight.

A six foot rattlesnake, the diamond markings on his bead-like back sharply etched, slithered across a rocky hump at the side of the trail. The reptile passed scarcely noticed. The eyes of the human intruders were lifted higher, were searching the buttes and the ledges and long running ridges for signs of greater danger.

Delgazin likely had given up. But they were entering an area where Apaches were more often encountered and each man was at keen alert. Guthry was minimizing possibilities all he could by sticking to the lesser trails where they would not be easily seen because of the multitude of rocks and bluffs. Vision would be impaired by the very nature of the country, and for them it was more a matter of listening for the enemy than of depending upon their eyes.

The heat was upon them almost from the moment the sun arose, and from then on built steadily with each minute until by mid-morning the sandstone and granite

132

that surrounded them gleamed with the sun's intensity and the temperature was edging close to a hundred degrees.

In this area not even the familiar, distorted shape of cholla cactus or wand like ocotillos were to be seen. A shriveled prickly pear now and then, an occasional yucca — and nothing else, since few things could find root purchase in the almost solid rock ground over which they were passing.

It was as if they were in a caldron, one heated from beneath by hell's own fires, further aided by the burning rays from the glowing ball hanging above.

"How — how much farther?" Erland Flood's voice had a desperate, pleading note.

Not wasting even the smallest measure of strength in order to look up, Guthry said: "Tomorrow — if we make it through today."

"Not sure I can . . . Heat's about got me."

"Worst part's now. Better later on — some."

Flood mopped at his streaming face. A fine dust had collected in his sweat soaked whiskers, lending him an odd, unearthly look. "Ought to stop — rest."

"Not here. Be like standing in a bonfire. Place farther on. Be a little shade. We'll pull up there."

He was thinking, too, of their jaded horses when he spoke. It was a small pocket adjacent to a tall monolith that blocked the sun early, began to lay a shadow not long after the mid-day hour. The ground was less rocky, and a stubby, tough grass had somehow found the will to spread a thin carpet of growth. It afforded grazing at its poorest, but it was something for the horses to work on.

"This Rich," Lot Maxwell said, "he been through here before?"

It was the first time Lot had broken silence since the day began. Guthry said: "Doubt it. Ask Severo. Could be he knows."

Lot repeated the question in Spanish. The old man, stolid, patient, seemingly changeless in the driving heat, shrugged. "I think not. He asked many questions of your father."

"Hard to figure how he could make it alone."

"He'll make it!" Erland Flood said in a strong voice. "The devil's spawn weathers all adversity, flourishes even. The righteous falter but to those with faith the Almighty grants strength to match the evildoer —"

"Wasn't asking for no sermon," Maxwell cut in wearily. "You ever a preacher, Marshal?"

"Farmer."

"Sound for sure like a preacher."

"A man can be filled with the spirit, with the word of God, and still be a farmer . . . Or a lawman."

Maxwell considered that in the sweltering silence. Then, "Reckon so, only your kind of yammering don't seem to jibe with wearing a badge."

"You're wrong! When told to be, we all become servants of the Almighty — become His right arm and carry out the commands He gives us."

Maxwell grunted. "Next thing you'll be saying it's wrong to kill a snake like this here Sul Rich."

134

Flood took his turn at being silent, apparently giving the question deep thought. "A man must pay for his sins," he said, finally. "It's right there in the Bible — an eye for an eye —"

"Then I've got a right to make him pay for murdering my folks — and Juan's grandson."

"Not you!" Flood shot back in a crackling tone. "Only by a man chosen by the Almighty can vengeance be taken upon the unworthy and —"

Lot Maxwell's laugh cut short the rush of words. "Meaning all lawmen are picked by the Almighty to do the avenging, that it?"

"The Almighty chooses —"

Guthry turned his attention from the senseless wrangling . . . They should be drawing near the formation where he planned to call a halt. He looked down the rockbound canyon-like section through which they were passing. Heat, in shimmering, blinding layers danced before his eyes. He narrowed his lids, endeavored to cut down the burning glare.

Motion . . . Guthry hissed a soft warning, lifted his hand to check the men behind him. Three Apaches rode across an opening between the boulders well to their left. All were slumped on their ponies, heads dropped forward, legs dangling loosely at the sides of their mounts.

"Didn't see us," Flood murmured.

Guthry nodded. "Damn lucky they didn't hear us, way you were carrying on. Could be others so keep it quiet."

135

They waited out another ten minutes under the brutal sun, moved on, Guthry now fully alert. They saw no more Indians and after a time he concluded the trio had been alone, likely were strays heading for some distant rendezvous.

An hour after that they reached the point where he planned to stop and drew in. Shade was beginning to inch its way out from the base of the high monument, and the grass looked even more scanty than he'd remembered. But there'd be some relief for both man and animal.

They remained there for a while, and then giving the horses a little water and treating themselves to a small quantity, pressed on, now quartering more directly into the west.

The ground was less rock studded here and the arroyos were giving way to small flats and saddles. The dust grew thicker, rose in clouds from the hooves of the lagging horses to settle upon the sweat soaked riders, cake their already saturated clothing until all appeared to be gray scarecrows wearing masks in which red-rimmed eyes and crusted lips were all that were visible.

Sundown came after an eternity of punishment; and when at last they pulled into the shadow of a butte where a few stunted cedars and a ragged stand of greasewood and mesquite made concealment fairly certain, all slid from their saddles with grateful sighs, so near total exhaustion they were scarcely conscious of their actions.

They lay sprawled on the yet hot sand for several minutes, Lot Maxwell still sufficiently aware to remain somewhat apart while the horses waited, heads down, legs spread for their riders to give them relief.

Dan Guthry stirred finally, struggled to his feet and, removing his gear from the big gelding, accorded him the usual ration of grain and water. The other men followed suit, each doing only what was necessary, and that slowly and with effort.

They would eat that night — and there'd be coffee, Guthry told himself with a grim sort of determination. Each of them was badly in need of a meal and the strength it would afford them. He'd build a small fire against the base of the butte, keep it shielded to kill the glare. They'd have fried meat, warmed and softened biscuits. Maybe he could uncover a can of peaches to be split among the four of them.

Only part of it came true. The Apaches had passed up the coffee beans, the biscuits. The meat, so carefully wrapped in oil paper, was gone. So also were the peaches. Wearily, he started the fire, put the lard tin of water over the flames, and turned to the others.

"Any of you got some jerky?"

Severo produced two short strips, Maxwell three. Flood had none. Taking what he had thrust into his own pocket, Dan dropped it all into the spider, poured a little water from their dwindling supply over it, and covered the pan with a tin plate.

"There will be no water until we come to the well in Ellenburg," the Mexican said, watching the preparations quietly.

137

"Be no Ellenburg unless we get something in our bellies," Guthry replied shortly.

Severo turned away. Guthry collected several of the biscuits, smashed them on a flat rock, dropped the chunks and crumbs into the frying pan with the meat. The contents began to simmer, set up a savory odor. He gauged the amount with a glance, added another cupful of their precious water.

It was probably their last meal until they reached the settlement; as well make enough, he thought, and looked then to the water boiling busily in the tin. Cupping a handful of crushed beans, he dumped them into the container, allowed the dark liquid to foam up, and then set it to one side.

It was cooler than usual, Dan decided, as he lay full length below the butte in the hush of darkness; or maybe it just seemed so. Things always appeared to be better when a man's hunger had been blunted by a full meal.

He yawned, stretched. A good night's sleep would make a difference, too — but they'd best not relax their vigilance. They were still in the land of the Apache.

Rising, he strolled to where the horses, hobbled, were nibbling at the thin grass. They'd be in better condition for the final miles to Ellenburg, too. Moving on, he climbed to the crest of a knoll, had his thorough look at the bleached, shadowed world around, saw nothing that gave cause for worry, and returned to camp.

Maxwell, Springfield across his knees, back resting against the slowly cooling face of the butte, eyed him narrowly and with suspicion. An arm's reach away Juan Severo also watched with studied care. Erland Flood slept. Reaching down, Dan shook the lawman to wakefulness.

"Let's make a try for that gun," he murmured as Flood looked up at him, and then moving on, he halted in front of Maxwell and Severo.

"No use telling you we're not out of the woods yet, far as the Apaches are concerned. Means we'll have to stand watch, same as before."

Maxwell said, "What I'm doing," and pointed to a shoulder of rock near the end of the bluff. "Can see good from there."

"Too much for one man — after a day like we've been through —"

"Juan'll be setting with me."

Flood was finally on his feet, edging toward the right. He was doing a poor job of making it all appear casual and without purpose.

"Doubt if two men can manage it. Easy to drop off, sleep. Could end up getting us caught again — or killed."

"If you're trying to euchre me into giving you the gun so's you can stand watch, forget it," Lot said flatly. "You plain ain't getting it."

"I'm interested in staying alive, damn it!" Guthry snarled, impatient with the slowness of the marshal. Flood had finally reached the end of the bluff. "You better listen to reason —"

Flood lunged awkwardly at Maxwell, giving no signal to Guthry. Instantly the younger man bounded to his feet. Shoulders pressed against the butte, he swung the rifle back and forth covering both lawmen. Dan swore deeply. The attempt might have succeeded if Flood had waited until he was a few steps closer, given him a chance to act also.

"Trying to trick me, eh?" Lot shouted, anger flashing in his eyes. "Get back — both of you — or one of you'll be dead!"

Guthry did not move. Flood turned away, walked slowly off. "Like I told you," Dan said, "somebody has to stay awake. Goes double for you now. I'll be watching. You give me half a chance I'll be on you with a rock, and I'll cave your head in . . . Keep thinking about that."

"You won't be getting the chance," Maxwell said sullenly.

"Don't take odds on it," Guthry snapped, and moved toward his blankets.

Settling down he watched Lot and Severo crawl up to the shoulder of rock, take positions back to back. There would be no getting the rifle now, he was certain of that, but there were still many miles to cross before they reached Ellenburg.

One thing was sure; the two men would do a good job of sentry duty. He could rest easy insofar as danger from prowling Apaches was concerned. The attempt to gain possession of the weapon had accomplished that much.

He lay down, closed his eyes, allowed his body to go lax. Nearby Deputy Marshal Flood was dropping off. Some men found sleep easy to come by . . . Seems he should — he was that tired . . . It was cooler . . . He was sure of it . . .

Something — a lizard or some other small creature of the night — dashing across Dan Guthry's face brought him awake. He sat up, glanced to the east. The first glare of light was beginning to show. He looked at Flood sleeping soundly, swung his attention then to the rock shoulder where Maxwell and Juan Severo had stationed themselves. Alarm shot through him. There was no sign of the two men.

Immediately he leaped to his feet, slapping at Flood as he did so. The lawman came up with a start.

"What —"

"Something's wrong. Don't see Lot or Severo anywhere."

The marshal scrambled to an upright position. "You think maybe the Indians come, got them?"

Dan Guthry shook his head slowly. He was looking at the horses. Only the sorrel and Flood's black were outlined in the half dark.

"Not the Apaches," he said heavily. "Lot and the Mexican have pulled out on us. Aim to beat us to Ellenburg and Sul Rich."

CHAPTER
SEVENTEEN

"No!"

Erland Flood's word of protest cracked like a shot in the morning hush. Dan Guthry did not hear, instead was snatching up his gear, hurrying toward the sorrel. Flood, a lean, agitated figure of outrage in the grayness, hung motionless for a long breath, and then recovering, followed quickly, began to saddle his horse.

Within a short time they were riding, threading their way through the narrow defiles, cool now but soon to be corridors of trapped, murderous heat; crossing broad flats and topping out low, sandy knolls. By the moment the sun pushed its molten shape above the eastern horizon they were well into the final leg of the Espantoso's smoldering length.

"Got to beat them," Flood muttered as they pressed on steadily. "Not the way it's to be — a stranger taking his life."

"It's the hangman's job," Guthry said, only half listening.

"There some way we can get to that town first? A short cut, maybe?"

142

"Not from here. Only hope we've got is that they don't find him right away — or that he's already pulled out."

Flood clawed at his whiskers nervously. "Can't let it happen . . . Not the will of the Almighty . . . Not the way He wants it."

Grim, Dan Guthry made no comment, simply stared ahead, squinting to see beyond the endless formations of wind carved sandstone and mounds of gray-brown earth. He was beginning to feel the lash of the terrible heat again.

The night's rest had restored his flow of vitality to a considerable extent, but he sensed a gradual eroding of his basic strength. Not entirely up to normal at the start of the journey because of the wounds he had sustained, he had begun the search at a disadvantage, although he would not admit such a fact to himself.

In times past he would have accepted the rigors of such a trip as this through the Espantoso as no more than a disagreeable, uncomfortable chore to be faced on a day by day footing. He was now looking forward to the end of the crossing and would welcome it gratefully.

Late in the morning they climbed out of the seething basin, saw in the distance the heat blurred green and gray that was Ellenburg. Immediately Guthry pulled to a stop. Erland Flood, anxious to reach the settlement as quickly as possible, sawed his horse around impatiently, glared at the younger lawman.

"Ain't no time to hold back! Ought to get there fast."

Dan shook his head. "Not from this side."

He raised himself in the stirrups, studied the town, endeavored to recall its layout.

"Maxwell and Severo will be keeping an eye on the road for us — if they haven't found Rich yet. And my guess is they haven't . . . Don't think they're much more'n an hour ahead of us."

"Then we sure ain't got no business stalling around —"

"We'll swing wide, come in from the east," Guthry said, ignoring the marshal. "They won't be watching that side."

Dan touched the sorrel with his spurs, and veering left to where he could drop down into a broad arroyo somewhat below the level of the land, moved out. Flood, seemingly undecided as to the necessity for such precautions, remained motionless for a time, and then followed.

Ellenburg was a sun and wind punished collection of two dozen or less structures lying on either side of a single street. A few dust sifted trees relieved the monotony of the landscape, and here, as in the Espantoso, heat was the governing factor of life and activity. No one stirred during the mid-day hours unless necessity was absolute.

When Dan Guthry and Flood rode up to the rear of the furthermost building, dismounted, paused long enough to give their horses a watering at a nearby trough, that aura of slumbering awareness hung over the place. Leaving the sorrel and the black to fend for themselves, they made their way along a passageway to

144

the front of its adjacent structure, and cautiously looked into the street. It was entirely deserted.

"One livery stable," Guthry said, taking quick stock along the roadway as he tucked the chained cuffs taken from his saddlebags into a hip pocket. "Makes it easy. If Sul Rich is still here that horse he stole will be there."

"Expect Maxwell and the Mexican fellow's thought of that, too."

"Doubt if they know what he was riding. Lot sure never saw it. Don't think Severo did either."

Dan moved out of the passageway alongside the building, brushed at the sweat clouding his eyes and crossed the street in long strides — a lean, dust-caked figure with grim, haggard features. Behind him Erland Flood hurried to keep up, his appearance made even more incongruous by the circular bush of matted gray-black whiskers masking his face.

They gained the stable, entered, felt at once the relief from the sun and heat in the thick walled structure's shadowy interior. Halting in the runway, Guthry glanced around. Several of the stalls to his right were occupied. There was no sign of a hostler. He bucked his head at the lawman.

"See if you can turn up somebody. I'll have a look at the horses."

The marshal moved away. Dan stepped into the first stall. A small buckskin — not the horse he sought. In the next compartment was an ancient gray, its bones sticking our prominently in a weathered hide. The third stall was empty.

145

Entering the fourth a sigh of satisfaction slipped from his lips. A tall bay, the Jay-Bar brand plain on its hips, slouched against the divider. This was the horse Henson had been riding and was later appropriated by Rich when, with Dan as hostage, he'd made his escape.

Guthry wheeled, a slow current of excitement and relief building within him. Despite everything — the Espantoso, the Apaches, Lot Maxwell and Juan Severo — they were not too late. Sul Rich was still in the settlement.

But he could be dead . . . Maxwell may have already called the outlaw to accounts. That thought sobered his spirits as he halted in the center of the runway to think. It wasn't likely Lot and Severo would carry out their plans there in the town. They'd take Rich, ride out . . . Voices at the rear of the barn brought him around. Flood had located the stable owner. Both were moving toward him — the marshal with a pistol in his hand.

"You find his horse?"

Dan nodded. "Bay there, with the Jay-Bar brand. See you got yourself a gun."

"Ruthered a had a rifle —"

Dan switched his attention to the hostler standing to one side, hands thrust deep into the pockets of his dirty, bibbed overalls.

"Got another one you'll sell?"

"Only iron I ever owned — never did use it none," the man replied. "Now, there's a gun shop down the street a piece. Hank Williams. Be sleeping this time a day, like I was, but you go around back and kick right smart on the door and I reckon he'll —"

146

"One's all we'll be needing," Flood broke in, thrusting the revolver into the waistband of his pants. "We better be getting to business."

The marshal was right. There was no time to be wasted. Guthry again faced the stableman. "Any idea where we can find the man who left that bay with you?"

The hostler shook his head. "Probably staying at the hotel. Ain't seen him since he first rode in."

"I know where he'll be," Erland Flood said in a firm voice. "This town got a bawdy house?"

The old hostler grinned. "Sure. Maggie's place. Down at the far end of the street. Sort of sets back, away from the others."

Surprised, Guthry stared at the marshal. "What makes you so sure he'll be there?"

"Know him — his kind. Always lay up in a place like that. Bad women — always looking for them."

Flood spun on a heel, and with Guthry at his side, started for the doorway. He had a hard set to his mouth and his eyes again had filled with intense, piercing lights.

Dan considered the lawman thoughtfully. Erland Flood had positive ideas about Sul Rich. It was almost as if he'd been well acquainted with the outlaw — yet he had denied the fact, or had done so in a general sort of way. A dull worry began to disturb Dan Guthry.

"You tell me you'd never met Sul Rich?"

The marshal's shoulders stirred. "Don't exactly recollect what I said. But they're all alike — helling around, sinning, drinking hard liquor — can figure on them always doing the same thing no matter —"

Guthry came to a halt, dropped his hand on Flood's arm. Beyond the open doorway, a short distance down the sun brilliant street, two men approached at a fast walk.

"Maxwell — and the Mexican fellow," the marshal muttered, catching sight of the pair at the identical instant. "Well, they ain't stopping me doing the Almighty's work! I'll fight them — make them —"

"Come on!" Guthry snarled, jerking the older man around. "We want no trouble with them."

CHAPTER
EIGHTEEN

Erland Flood planted his booted feet stubbornly on the littered floor of the stable, shook off Guthry and dropped a hand to the pistol in his waistband.

"I ain't turning back!"

"You looking for a shoot-out with Maxwell, that it?" Guthry demanded angrily. "That's what it'll be. He'll fight you sure as hell to get at Rich."

"Can't let nobody stand in the way of the Almighty's justice. I've got the power to kill if need be."

Again Guthry seized Flood's arm. "What kind of a lawman are you?" he demanded. "We've got no quarrel with Lot Maxwell — leastwise none big enough to shoot him down."

"The law of the Alm —"

"They haven't found Sul yet, else they wouldn't be coming here. Probably been through all the saloons, now aim to ask the hostler about any strangers riding in. That'll give us a chance to cut them out for good."

The relentless stance of Erland Flood wavered. "Meaning what?"

"We'll trap them," Dan said, and whirled to the hostler. Pointing to the small office in the rear of the building, he snapped: "In there — hurry!"

The older man frowned, hesitated. "What the hell for?"

Guthry gave him a hard shove. "I'm a sheriff," he rasped, lifting the flap of his shirt pocket. "Man with me is a U.S. marshal. That's all you need to know. Now, do what you're told or you're in plenty of trouble!"

"Yes — yes, sir," the hostler stammered, eyes spreading with surprise. "What d'you want me to do?"

"Get inside your office. There'll be two men come in here. When they sing out for you, call them back, get them inside. And keep them in there. Understand?"

"Sure. But why —"

"Reason won't mean anything to you," Dan said, again pushing the hostler toward the doorway of the small room.

"We'll be waiting right outside. Don't want them to know we're here. Remember that."

The stableowner stepped into his quarters. Dan pulled back into the darkness behind a pile of straw, motioned Flood into the shadows beyond him. He gave the marshal a close look, said: "Forget that pistol. You won't be needing it."

Lot Maxwell, rifle in the crook of his arm, walked into the opening at the far end of the runway, Severo at his side. The Mexican veered off, began to look into the stalls. Lot brushed his hat to the back of his head, sleeved away the sweat.

"Hostler!" he shouted, glancing around. "Anybody here?"

There was a pause, and then the stableman answered. "Here . . . Come on back."

Maxwell replaced his headgear, beckoned to Severo and together they walked the remaining length of the barn, halting just outside the small office.

"Asking about a man riding in," Lot said. "Would've been yesterday, maybe the day before. Red-headed fellow. Come from the Espantoso."

The hostler tugged at his nose. "Well, been a couple of strangers show up. Don't exactly know where they come from."

Impatience stirred Guthry. He wanted Lot and Juan Severo inside the room, not outside talking. That damned hostler wasn't doing what he'd been told . . . It could come down to Flood's pistol yet.

"Come on in," the stableman said in his whining voice, "let me do some thinking on it."

Maxwell entered the room. Severo hesitated briefly, and then removing his hat, followed. Instantly Guthry glided from his place behind the straw. Grabbing the edge of the door, he slammed it shut, dropped the iron pin in the hasp.

A startled oath went up inside the room. A hand tried the door, lightly at first, and then with sudden force.

"Won't hold them long," Guthry said. "Let's go."

Wheeling, he strode swiftly up the runway to the entrance. Without hesitating, he turned into the still deserted street, struck for the far end and the house the hostler had designated.

Flood caught up with him after the first three strides, moved shoulder to shoulder with him, his bearded face, where visible, glistening with sweat. The old lawman walked with a heavy footed solidness, a sort of irresistible determination that made it appear nothing short of a bolt from the heavens would halt him now in his purpose.

Guthry eyed the older man with growing concern. "I want him alive, Marshal. Remember that."

Flood grunted. They moved on down the roadway, Dan aware of a face now and then peering at them through dust filmed windows, some with curiosity, others in surprise. Idly he noted the names of the neglected appearing stores: BonTon Bakery, Gilsdorf's Feed & Grain, the Apache Cafe, Bannerman's Saloon, the Espantoso Basin Bank . . .

Did Ellenburg have a lawman? If so, he and Flood should first report there, make known their identities and the purpose of their visit. Professional courtesy demanded such. But there was not time for the amenities now; later, when it was all over and Sul Rich was cuffed in irons and ready for transporting back to Lawsonville, he'd seek out the town's lawman, explain.

"There he comes . . . "

Guthry pulled up short beside Flood. He saw Sul Rich move from the rear entrance of a sagging, two storied old residence at the farther edge of a vacant lot a hundred yards away. Flood had guessed right about the outlaw, had known exactly where the man would be found.

"Headed this way — for the alley," Dan said. "Probably going for the back door of one of the saloons."

152

He swiveled his attention to the right. A few steps ahead a narrow, weed littered passage separating two adjacent buildings offered a solution.

"Through there," he said in a tight voice. "We can head him off."

Moving quickly, he entered the shadowed corridor, stifling with trapped heat, hurried down its length to the lower end of the structures. Behind him he could hear Erland Flood trampling heavily through the trash, making no effort at silence.

"Easy," he hissed over his shoulder.

Reaching the corner of the building to his left, Dan removed his hat, peered around into the alley. A grim satisfaction filled him. Rich, his ruddy face much darker than before, reddish hair raggedly covering his neck, clothing bleached and worn, was coming straight for them. The outlaw's head was tipped down, eyes on the dusty ground before him. He suspected nothing.

An unreasonable and wholly unaccountable anger boiled through Dan Guthry suddenly . . . *I've got you, you sonofabitch — got you cold . . . I've come a long way for this and when I'm done with you I'm taking you back to hang . . . Even if I have to carry you on my back!*

Just as quickly the surging fury passed and he once again was calm and coolly calculating the moments ahead. He glanced along the alley. A small shed was immediately opposite them. Grab Rich, rush him into the sagging old structure where they could not be seen; there, with his fists, enjoy a few minutes of personal restitution for the vile action Rich had inflicted upon him back in the sandy coulee near Lawsonville, then slap the cuffs on him. Such could all be neatly accomplished without the residents of Ellenburg being the wiser.

Half turning, he touched Flood's arm, pointed to the shed. "We hustle him into there — then you stand back, watch the door. Got a little business of my own to look after."

The marshal nodded, drew his pistol.

"Not that," Guthry warned. "He's no good to anybody dead."

The harsh scuff of boot heels on the baked earth silenced further words. Dan swung his attention back to the alley, crouched, cat-like, to spring. Abruptly Sul Rich was before him.

Guthry launched himself at the outlaw. His head-on rush caught Sul from the side, jolted breath from him, set him to staggering. Driving hard, Dan carried the man off balance before him, knocked him into the shed.

Rich crashed into the back wall of the small structure. He rebounded, went to his knees, hand grabbing frantically for the pistol on his hip. He came up with it fast. Guthry kicked out, sent the weapon flying into a far corner, and swinging, smashed his fist into the outlaw's jaw.

Dazed, Sul Rich sank back, stared at the lawman in amazement. And then as he looked beyond Guthry, his mouth sagged and his eyes widened in greater surprise.

154

"Hellhound!" The word ripped from Erland Flood's lips, seemingly echoed in the small shed. "Been better if I'd throttled you the day you was borned!"

Dan Guthry saw the look of astonishment on the outlaw's features change into bitter hatred, and then as the marshal's words drilled into his own consciousness, he wheeled to face the man who had been at his side from Lawsonville.

In a single, flashing instant everything became clear. What a fool he'd been! All that crazy talk the man he'd accepted as Erland Flood had spouted; his disclaimed but uncanny knowledge of Sul Rich, his fierce determination to press the search, bring down the outlaw he said he'd been commanded to punish ... Guthry had no idea what had happened to the real Erland Flood, but one thing was certain, this man with him was no U.S. marshal, he was Sul Rich's father!

"Pa!"

The sound from Sul Rich was a strangled gasp, and in that same breath Dan Guthry realized that not only was his prisoner's life in jeopardy but his own as well. He pivoted to one side, grabbed for the pistol he'd kicked from the outlaw's hand, caught it up, came back around.

He had a quick glimpse of two burning eyes, a distorted face buried in sweat and dust clotted whiskers, and then something crashed into his head and he plunged downward into blackness.

CHAPTER
NINETEEN

Dan Guthry returned to consciousness with the rumble of a deep voice in his ears . . . Erland Flood — no, it was Amos Rich; he remembered what the records had said: Amos Rich, father. Mary Rich, mother. Both dead. That was what Sul had told him when he was filling out the papers. He stirred, found himself bound hand and foot. A gag pulled tight across his lips was making it difficult to breathe.

Clearing away the last of the mist, he fixed his eyes on the two figures in the dimness of the shed. Amos Rich was bending over his son, and the thought: he's killed him already, passed through the lawman's mind. But as Amos straightened up he saw he was wrong; the older man had been in the act of tying the outlaw's ankles together.

"My bounden duty," Amos Rich said stubbornly. "Word come down to me from the Almighty."

"The hell!" Sul snarled. "You're crazier than you ever were . . . I'm your own flesh and blood. You can't do it."

"If a man's right eye offends him pluck —"

"Don't give me that crap," the outlaw began and then settled back, a slyness coming over him. "Maybe

I've been bad, Pa, but you can't do what you say . . . It's wrong, all wrong . . . You think about it."

"I've done that — thought about it for a long time. The way you are, what you turned out to be, James Sullivan. Don't see why the Almighty didn't take you when you was borned, spared me and your ma all that pain and trouble you give us."

"I tried, Pa, honest I did," the outlaw said in a penitent voice. "Reckon I just wasn't strong as you. I always meant to —"

"Spawn of the devil — that's what you are," the older man rumbled on as if not hearing. "Never was no good in you, only bad. Plain rottenness . . . Should've done something about it myself instead of waiting for the Almighty to tell me I had to fix things right."

"Fix things — you mean kill me?"

"What I mean. The Almighty made me see my duty. Get you from His sight, He said. Rid His earth of you. Was me responsible for you drawing the first breath of life. Up to me now to end it — end you."

"You do that, Pa, and you'll be bad as you claim I am."

"No, I'm a God fearing man doing what's right. And I'm strong — strong enough to heed the voice of the Almighty when He tells me I've got to do it, even if it be my own son I'm killing."

"And that won't make you a sinner?"

"I'm a plain man, doing what I been told."

"You'll be a killer, same as me . . . And that U.S. marshal you knocked in the head — you figure that was all right, too? The Almighty tell you to do that?"

157

"Was all in the doing of my duty. Ain't no man can figure the ways of the Almighty, and it ain't fitten to question them. He sent word down to me where you was being held — locked up — for murdering some folks. Told me I was to go there, take your life, James Sullivan, because it was me who gave you life ... What evil a man makes, he must also destroy, else he, too, will suffer the everlasting fires of damnation!"

Feigning unconsciousness, Dan Guthry listened to the droning voice of Amos Rich as he rambled on. The picture was clear now. In his twisted mind Amos had become convinced that he was heaven-sent to personally execute his own son in order to wash himself clean of the sense of guilt that rode him. In the process of this cold-blooded plan, he had waylaid the real Deputy Marshal Erland Flood, assumed his identity. It was evident that what he had done and would do in the future was considered by him as a sacred duty.

In the breathlessly hot confines of the shed, Sul Rich struggled briefly against his bonds. Amos stood over him, staring down — a motionless, vengeful figure in the dimness.

"It's the will of the Almighty," he intoned.

The outlaw spat, swore feelingly. Pointing with his chin at Guthry, he said, "Killing him a part of your orders, too?"

Amos turned his attention to Dan. "A good man — a real good one, but there ain't no way out of it. It's the scheme of the Almighty."

"Makes you one up on me then, Pa. I ain't never killed a lawman. You kill him, that makes you better'n me . . . How you figure to do it?"

The slyness had returned to the outlaw's manner. He lay quiet, his small, hooded eyes half closed, lips pulled down as he studied his parent.

"We're going into the desert — the three of us," Amos Rich said. "There I'll rid myself of him — and you. Then it'll be done with, and the Almighty'll be pleased."

"What about you? What'll you do after that?"

"Go back to the farm, work the land."

"You'll never make it, Pa. Take it from me — I know. They'll be after you, dogging you every step."

"Who will?" the old man asked blankly.

"Other lawmen. People themselves. You can't just up and kill a U.S. marshal —"

"Never killed him, only knocked him out, tied him up —"

"Well, you're aiming to kill this sheriff. All the same. You can't just ride off after doing something like that. The Almighty ought've told you that."

"He'll protect me, same as He has others —"

"He won't get no chance. They'll track you down, hang you higher'n a hawk's nest before you know what's going on! Listen to me, Pa. Listen real good because I know what I'm talking about. Bust in that sheriff's head right now, leave him laying here in the shed — and then let's you and me line out for Mexico. Ain't far from here, no more'n thirty miles. Once we're over the border ain't nobody who can touch us."

"The Almighty can — and he'll know about me. He'll look down and say I ain't done what I was told."

"Forget the Almighty! He can't help you now. You're a dead man, Pa, unless you do what I say."

"There ain't no running away from the Almighty, James Sullivan. You ought to know that."

"Not Him I'm worrying about . . . Go get us a couple of horses. Nobody'll notice you. Folks around here don't stir much until sundown. We can be a far piece from this old shed by the time somebody finds the sheriff — and then it'll be too late for them to take out after us."

Amos Rich brushed wearily at his face, turned, stared through the doorway into the glaring world outside. "Word of the Almighty's got to be obeyed," he mumbled. "I'm getting horses but not for what you said. I aim to fulfill the word of the Almighty — clean my hands of your sinning. And it'll be done where only He can witness my disgrace."

Sul groaned in disgust, swore again. Dan Guthry, arms behind his back, had been working steadily at the cord Amos Rich had tied about his wrists. He was making some headway, it seemed, but he was not sure; it could be only slack.

He was thankful for one thing. Amos had either forgotten or overlooked the iron cuffs he carried in his rear pocket. Had the old man made use of them the desperate situation he was in would be utterly hopeless.

"Better listen to me, Pa," Sul Rich said, taking up the plea again. "Forget the sheriff — get us a couple of

160

horses and let's make a run for the border. Its your only chance."

"Only chance," Amos echoed woodenly. "Only chance for me to undo all the wrong I've caused is to take your life, James Sullivan. Me — not the law. Not the puny law of men, but by obeying the law of the Almighty. That's my only chance."

Abruptly he pulled the dust filled bandana from about his neck, took a long step forward. Bending over, he tied it tight across the outlaw's mouth.

"I won't be gone long," he said in a voice that was almost kind as he straightened up. "Just you be patient, son."

Amos Rich moved to the doorway of the shed, paused there to look up and down the alley. A curious feeling of release was pouring through him, filling him with ease, calming his mind and setting him at peace with the world and all things in it.

The end of the journey was at hand. He was on the threshold of fulfilling the task with which the Almighty, in His all-seeing wisdom, had entrusted him. It was a good feeling, and he wished Mary were alive to share the moments of redemption and triumph that lay ahead for him. She could rejoice with him in the knowledge that he was at last making right the wrong they, together, had cast upon the world.

But she would know it. The Almighty would tell her. He'd pat her on the shoulder, assure her that she no longer need feel shame, that her husband, in spite of all obstacles, had carried out His will.

The trash cluttered alley was deserted. At the far end he recognized the stable where Guthry had found James Sullivan's horse, and where they had locked the Mexican fellow and Lot Maxwell in the hostler's quarters.

Lot Maxwell . . . And the Mexican fellow . . .

He'd forgotten about them. They could cause trouble. Best he go careful until he could tell if they were still in the stableman's room. If so, all well and good; if not — Amos shrugged, looked to see if the pistol he'd purchased was still under his waistband. It was. He bobbed his head in satisfaction, stepped into the open. He reckoned he'd just have to use the weapon on Lot and the Mexican fellow if they interfered . . . Why couldn't folks get it in their heads that they couldn't stand in the way of the Almighty!

Keeping close to the rear of the buildings, he made his way to the livery barn. Halting at the back entrance, he listened. All was quiet inside. Either the men had managed to break out, or had given up, settled down to wait for someone to come along, release them.

Grasping the weathered door, Amos opened it slowly. It swung limply, its improvised hinges made from old harness leather allowing the bottom edge to drag against the ground. Moving silently, he entered, crossed the manure packed floor to the runway and halted. The door to the hostler's quarters was open, the hasp sticking rigidly out from the splintered frame work.

They had managed to escape. Amos considered that, all the while listening into the gloom of the barn. He could hear only the munching of the horses, an

162

occasional thud as one shifted. The place was deserted, he decided. Probably the hostler had gone with Maxwell and the Mexican fellow, and all were searching for him and Sheriff Guthry. That was good — only it brought up a new problem.

He and Guthry had left their horses at the rear of a building on the opposite side of the street. To cross over would be taking a big risk — a mighty big one. Someone maybe would see him. He glanced along the stalls, sighed. He reckoned there was no problem after all. He'd simply use three of the horses he saw there.

Moving to the first compartment, he pulled the saddle from the divider, threw it into place, drew the cinch tight and reached for the bridle, all the while muttering softly to the horse. That chore finished, he stepped into the next stall. James Sullivan's horse, he noted. He'd do fine. He chose a buckskin for the third mount, mostly because the gear for it was handy, and he didn't want to tarry in the barn any longer than necessary; that hostler, and maybe Maxwell and the Mexican fellow just might return.

The horses ready, he backed them into the runway, and gathering the reins in his hand, led them out the back into the alley. Down the way a piece a woman was walking slowly across her yard but she paid him no mind and he continued, again keeping close to the rear of the buildings and moving leisurely.

When he reached the shed, he circled to the back. As he looped the reins into the branches of a stunted cedar, he had a look at the surrounding country. A fairly deep arroyo running parallel to the alley lay only a dozen paces away, placed there by Providence, he was certain. By riding down into it, they could depart the settlement without fear of being seen by anyone who happened to glance that way.

Satisfied that everything was going just as it should, he turned, moved back to the doorway of the shed.

CHAPTER
TWENTY

Dan Guthry heard Rich's heavy step outside the shed, saw the opening darken as the man's bulk filled the doorway. Anxious, he worked at the cords binding his wrists. He'd managed to slide the knot around to where he could pick at it with the fingernails of his right hand. It was loosening; he now was sure.

"Horses're ready," Amos said, ignoring Dan. "Now, James Sullivan, we're walking out and climbing aboard real quiet like. You make a fuss I'll just have to bash you over the head. You hear me?"

Sul nodded violently, tried to speak. Amos crossed to where he sprawled, pulled the gag down.

"You saying something?"

"Just trying to say you'd be needing help, Pa, loading up the sheriff and such. Best you untie my hands."

Amos Rich grinned toothily. "You taking me for some kind of a fool, boy? I've been on to your cunning ways for years." He paused, glanced at Guthry. "Reckon it will take some doing, however . . . Twist your back to me."

Sul complied hastily, eagerly. Amos squatted down, removed the cord from the outlaw's wrists.

"Now, put them back together — front side," he directed.

The outlaw frowned. "But, Pa —"

"You heard me! I ain't setting you loose, I'm just tying your hands in front instead of in the back. That way you can help me."

Sul glared at the older man, and his body seemed to tense. Amos shrugged, reached for the pistol in his waistband. "Mind what I said about putting up a fuss," he warned.

The outlaw swore sullenly, laid his wrists together, watched as his father rebound them with the cord.

"Now, take that rope off'n your feet while I get the sheriff ready."

"Ain't much sense in that," Sul observed. "He ain't done no moving. Expect he's already dead — or most."

Amos pivoted, peered at Guthry. "He's still a breathing," he said, and began to pluck at the length of rope binding the lawman's ankles. "Expect I'd better leave his gag be," he added, and reaching up, shook Dan's shoulder roughly. "Sheriff — you hear me? Want you to stand on your feet."

Guthry, back placed close to the wall to hide his hands, nodded groggily. As if barely able he struggled to an upright position. Sul had discarded his leg bonds, was also getting to his feet. Amos jerked a thumb at the door.

"Horses're out behind the shed."

Dan felt the elder Rich's hand drop on his shoulder, wheel him about, guide him into the blinding sunlight. Something thumped against him and, from the tail of

166

an eye he saw it was Sul, that Amos had him imprisoned in his grasp, also.

They came to the corner of the shed. The horses, Dan saw, were not theirs. Amos was as smart as he was addled; he'd taken no chances on being seen by going after the sorrel and the black, had stayed out of sight and simply appropriated from the stalls in the stable.

Such could backfire on the old man; it was plain and simple horse theft, but Dan doubted it would matter. By the time the owners discovered their loss — no earlier than dark, probably — he'd be dead along with Sul, and Amos Rich would be far away.

"Still telling you you're making a mistake," Sul grumbled. "You oughtn't to be bothering with this here sheriff. He'll just slow us down . . . You loan me that gun you got and I'll work over his head and we'll leave him laying there in that wash. Then we can head out fast for Mexico."

"We ain't going to Mexico," Amos said angrily. "You quit thinking that! I'm taking you and him out on the desert, doing what I been told to do . . . Get a hold there, help me boost him onto the saddle."

Together the two men hoisted Guthry to the buckskin's back. Amos said: "It sure wouldn't be smart to leave him laying around here. Supposing somebody happened along right after we pulled out. Then we'd have somebody trailing us quick. I take him along, like I'm doing, nobody'll ever know we've even come — and went . . . Get on your horse, James Sullivan."

Amos stood back, waited while Sul climbed onto his saddle, and then attaching lead ropes to both Guthry's and the outlaw's horses, swung onto his own mount. Holding the leads in his left hand, he rode down into the arroyo, the bay and the buckskin side by side, following.

Swaying, maintaining the appearance of being only partly conscious, Dan Guthry tore persistently at the knot in the cord binding his wrists. He was sweating freely, having difficulty also with his breathing as the gag shut off some of the air he normally would intake.

He felt the cords give as an end came free, slid a glance at Sul, an arm's length to his right. The outlaw was staring moodily ahead. He hadn't noticed anything, and Amos Rich, a short distance in the lead, was studying the burning land. Carefully, Dan flexed his hands, applying pressure. The cord slipped a half inch, drew taut. Almost, but not quite . . . A little more time.

"Was lucky I found you first, James Sullivan," Amos said, breaking the lengthy silence. "Reckon you didn't know that Lot Maxwell and his Mexican friend was looking for you, too."

"Maxwell?" Sul repeated, clearly surprised.

"Son of them homesteaders you up and killed. Now, he's the kind of son I wisht you'd a been. A good boy, looking out for his folks, not troubling them and putting your ma in her grave and filling me with shame, way you done. A real fine son, that Lot Maxwell. A credit to his folks."

"Didn't know they had a son," Sul replied. "You say he was in town looking for me?"

168

"Aiming to kill you, too — him and the Mexican fellow. Severo, name is. Grandpa of that little boy you went and shot down. Why'd you do a thing like that, James Sullivan? He was only a younker. Never could've done you no harm."

Sul laughed. "Was sort of funny like. I got done taking care of the old man and his woman. Was looking for some money and they kept saying they didn't have none. Finally decided they didn't so I cut down on them . . . Then I seen this here kid legging it for the barn."

"Put me in mind of a little old prairie dog a scooting for his hole. There was two bullets left in the gun I'd took off the sheriff there, so I up and cracked down on the kid . . . Knocked him ass over appetite! Sure was a funny sight. Kept me laughing all day."

Hardened lawman that he was Dan Guthry recoiled in revulsion at the outlaw's insensate words. Sul Rich was utterly ruthless, without a trace of conscience in his warped soul. For the first time in his life Dan Guthry understood lynch law and the feelings that motivated mobs when they were dealing with men such as Sul Rich. Law was law — but was there a time when the gallows was too good for a criminal?

And Amos Rich, distorted and crippled in mind in a different way, was equally as bad. He was the unbalanced, self proclaimed minion-of-God sort, following his narrow rut blindly, scything all who had the misfortune to find themselves in his way. Which was worse? The coldblooded, unfeeling gunman who acted

169

out of impulse, or the zealot who felt himself possessed with righteousness?

It was a difficult question to answer, Dan thought, and he'd be another of their victims if he couldn't free himself soon. Even then he'd be dependent upon luck; with no weapon Amos Rich would still hold the upper hand.

"You always was that way," the older Rich was saying. "Mean. Just pure mean. Was no call for you to kill that boy. And doing it was the worst thing you could've done, far as the Almighty's concerned . . . Younkers are sort of special with him . . . Suffer little children to come unto me — you remember the Lord saying that, James Sullivan?"

"Well, you ought. You was told that, plenty of times. But what'd you do — go right ahead and kill one, just like it meant nothing. There just ain't no good in you at all . . . I'll swear, James Sullivan, I don't know where all that bad blood come from."

"Me neither, Pa . . . We keep heading south like we are, won't be long before we'll come to Mexico —"

"We ain't going to Mexico. Only place you're going is to hell, James Sullivan. You're going to pay for all the bad things you done. You're going to suffer torments just the way the Almighty says you have to. You'd best be getting yourself fixed and ready. You recollect how to pray?"

"I remember, only it's kind of hard with my hands tied the way they are. Maybe, if you was to cut the cord so's I can put my hands together —"

170

"Ain't no need for that. Just you bow your head and start talking. The Almighty'll know you're praying and'll start listening." Amos paused, looked back over his shoulder toward Ellenburg, now little more than a shimmering mirage in the blazing heat, and then glanced ahead to a run of low bluffs.

"Reckon that'll be a good place to hold the services. Quiet and peaceful like, and far enough from town so's nobody'll hear the shooting."

Straining, Guthry threw his strength against the cord. It fell free. He felt his wrists separate, checked the movement quickly, fearful of drawing attention from Sul. The outlaw was absorbed in contemplation of the not too distant bluffs.

"Pa," he said after a time, "did ma ever talk about me — after I run off, I mean?"

"Now and then. Was usually on the Sabbath. Wanted you mentioned in the praying we done."

"Did you?"

"Once in a while, at first. Then didn't seem no use. But I got to thinking later, after your ma died, that maybe I'd faulted there. Maybe if I'd prayed harder you'd a turned from your evil ways and quit doing the bad things I'd heard said about you."

"Reckon I failed the Almighty there, too. I should've kept right on trying. It sure is a terrible thing knowing you've failed the Almighty, son . . . Like a powerful big burden a-setting on your shoulders, bearing down on you."

"But this'll put things right. I'll be doing what's expected of me — sacrificing my own flesh and blood,

171

just like folks done in the olden times when they wanted to please the Almighty."

You've got your ropes crossed, old man, Guthry thought, looking toward the bluffs only yards away now. When they halted he'd get off the saddle quick before Amos could come to lend him a hand, and perhaps note the cord loose on his wrists. He'd try then to get a grip on the chain linked cuffs in his back pocket. When the older man moved in close, he'd swing fast, straight for the head. With luck he'd end up with the pistol.

"Reckon there's a nice place," Amos Rich said, pulling to a halt. He pointed to the sandy face of the bluff. "You go over there and set yourself down and wait a bit, James Sullivan. Best I take care of the sheriff first . . . Then we'll hold our services . . . "

Taut, Guthry threw one leg over the saddle, dropped to the ground, arms still held behind his body. Amos nodded genially, watched Sul dismount, and then came off his own horse. Pistol in hand, he moved toward Dan.

"Glad to know you're feeling better, Sheriff . . . Now, I'm real sorry for what I got to do —"

Guthry swung the iron cuffs in a swift arc. The end circle caught Amos Rich just below the left cheekbone. He yelled, staggered back, dropped the revolver.

Dan lunged for the weapon. Sul Rich was there before him, on his knees, scooping up the pistol with both hands.

"You crazy old psalm-singing bastard!" he yelled, and fired twice in quick succession.

172

Amos Rich jolted from the impact of the heavy bullets, spun half about, fell. Guthry, surging forward, flung out an arm, caught Sul with his outstretched fingers and dragged him down.

The pistol exploded again, making an odd muffled noise as it drove the bullet into the loose sand beneath the outlaw. Dan struck hard with a balled fist at Sul's face, using one of the cuffs to supplement his knuckles. The blow landed on the outlaw's jaw, cracked sharply. Sul's head snapped to one side and his eyes rolled wildly.

Guthry's left hand closed about the pistol, wrenched it free. He struck again, this time with greater force. Sul Rich stiffened, began to quiver. Gasping for wind, Dan tore the partly displaced gag from his mouth, sat for a brief time, body heaving, sweat flowing from every pore while he sucked in the clean, hot air.

Then, leaning forward, he snapped the iron circles around the outlaw's wrists, not troubling to remove the cord that already bound them. He glanced at the pistol, swore, and tossed it aside. The barrel, thrust into the sand when Sul triggered the last shot, had burst. He was still without a weapon . . . But maybe it was all over now . . . Maybe he wouldn't need one.

Rising, he took the half dozen steps to where Amos Rich lay, bearded face up, sightless eyes staring into the molten sun. The first bullet had been enough. The second one discharged by Sul had been from pure hate.

Wearily, Guthry turned, undecided as to his next move. Ellenburg was out of the question. He'd never get Rich past it alive — not with Maxwell and Juan

Severo still waiting; and he had no heart for facing the Espantoso again, anyway.

The settlement on the border. He tried to recall what he knew of the place — its name, if it had a lawman. His mind refused to function. Angrily, he brushed at the sweat on his face and neck . . . Best go there, regardless; he could get help of some kind.

Small dots moving through the dancing heat waves in the distance brought him to attention. Two riders coming up fast from the direction of Ellenburg . . . They could only be Lot Maxwell and the Mexican, Severo.

CHAPTER
TWENTY-ONE

They had been seen riding from Ellenburg, Dan realized, and Maxwell and Severo, searching relentlessly for them, had turned up that information. Now, once more he had them to contend with — and he was again unarmed.

"On your horse!" he snarled at Sul Rich in a sudden gust of frustration and anger.

The outlaw staggered to his feet, rubbing at his jaw. He saw the distant riders and his eyes narrowed.

"Them the two pa was talking about?"

Guthry, jerking the lead ropes free of Amos Rich's saddle, nodded. At once Rich turned to his mount, pulled himself aboard. Dan swung to the buckskin, and digging spurs into the horse and shouting at the outlaw's bay, broke the two horses into a quick lope.

"Where we headed?" Rich flung the question at him.

"South — for that border town."

Dan glanced over his shoulder. Lot and Severo had altered course, were angling across the heat swept flat hoping to trim the distance that separated them by following a direct line. Guthry urged the buckskin to a faster pace.

"Keep that horse moving!" he shouted to Rich. "Outrun them is all we can do. I've got nothing to hold them off with."

Smirking, Sul crouched lower over his horse, apparently enjoying some secret knowledge. They dropped into a long wash, crossed, rode in behind a row of gray and red tinted bluffs. Immediately they were lost to view of Maxwell and Juan Severo. Guthry, seizing the opportunity, altered course, struck an almost due east direction. The outlaw raised himself on the saddle, narrow face drawn into a frown.

"This ain't the way to Escabosa!" he called in a protesting voice.

"It's the way we're going!" Guthry shot back, holding tight to the bay's lead rope.

He understood now what had lain in the outlaw's dark mind — even as far back as the shed where they had both been captives of Amos Rich. He had friends in the border town, ones he could depend upon for help. Reaching there he would have had things all his way.

The lawman gave him his own sly smile. "You won't be getting away from me again — not alive."

The smirk was again on the outlaw's features. "We'll see, Sheriff!" he answered. "The ball ain't over yet."

"For you it is," Guthry said.

But victory lay only on the surface. Avoiding the settlement of Escabosa left him entirely at a loss as to any definite plan. Where did the next town lie? He hadn't the slightest idea. The only advantage gained in changing directions was the added possibility of losing

176

the two men on their trail — and that could prove temporary.

An hour later they topped out onto a high plateau. Guthry looked back as the horses pounded on. Maxwell and Juan Severo were small specks far to the southwest. They would see him and Rich now, change course also. But he'd picked up a good lead, one easily maintained if they encountered no bad luck.

It struck late in the afternoon. Eyes on a not too distant cloud of smoke or dust — he couldn't be sure which — Dan was letting the buckskin have his head as they moved on at a steady lope. The men behind them had managed to close the gap to some extent, but they were still at a safe distance, assuming a settlement could be located.

Suddenly the buckskin stumbled, went down. Guthry soared over the horse's head, but he clung grimly to the lead rope fastened to the bay Sul Rich rode. He landed hard on his left shoulder, felt a blinding shock of pain as his barely healed arm took the brunt of the spill.

Dazed as he was, he was up and on his feet instantly, ignoring the pain, intent only upon retaining possession of his prisoner. Rich, hands linked by both cord and chains, fought to drive the bay over him, wheeling the horse in a tight circle, sawing savagely on the reins. But Guthry managed to get a hand on the bay's headstall, haul him down.

Rich grinned at the sweating lawman. "Next time," he murmured.

Guthry threw a hasty glance at the buckskin. The horse had stepped in a gopher hole, stood now head low, favoring his right foreleg. He was done for. Dan looked then to Maxwell and Severo. They were coming on fast. At once he crossed to Rich, and swinging up behind him, wrenched the reins from his hands. The outlaw cursed.

"This nag ain't going far carrying double," he protested.

"You better hope he goes far enough," Guthry snapped, and roweled the bay into motion.

It was dust — not smoke. This became clear to Dan Guthry a short time later when they reached the rim of the mesa, dropped off onto a long slope . . . And it was not a settlement, merely a stagecoach rest stop.

A solitary tree, a single wooden structure with a water tank. He could see a coach with its four horse span standing in the yard, the driver perched high on the box. There were no signs of passengers; either they were inside the vehicle or were taking brief ease from the rigors of their journey within the shack.

Guthry's jaw was set to hard lines as he swung the fast fading bay into the hard packed yard and pulled up beside the coach. Two men appeared in the doorway of the building at the sound of the bay's hooves, peered out curiously. The driver, shifting the cud in his mouth, looked down, his leathery features screwed into a frown.

Guthry leaped from the bay, dragged Rich after him. Reaching for the handle of the coach door, he yanked it open, shoved the outlaw roughly onto the cushion. Pivoting, he faced the driver.

"Pull out!" he shouted.

The old man stared down from his lofty seat. "Hell, I got pass —"

"Pick them up later!" Guthry snarled. He jerked back the flap of his pocket, pushed his star forward for the driver to see. "This is law business. Get your rig to rolling!"

The driver bobbed his head, slapped at his team with the slack in the reins. The coach leaped into motion as the horses lunged against the harness. Guthry caught the edge of the door frame, heaved himself into the dust powdered interior of the vehicle.

Back at the way-stop the two men were running into the yard, waving their arms frantically and yelling, but their words were lost to the hammering of the horses and the creaking and groaning of the coach as it got under way.

Dan raised his glance to the rim of the mesa. Maxwell and Severo had not reached that point as yet. By the time they arrived at the shack and learned what had taken place, it would be too late for them to do anything. He reckoned he'd shaken them for good, finally.

Settling back on the seat, he allowed his breathing to become normal, his taut body to relax. Through the spinning particles of dust Sul Rich faced him from the opposite bench, his face still wearing the same smirking insolence.

"Working up a lot of sweat for nothing, Sheriff," he drawled. "You'll never get me back to that two-bit rat hole you call a town."

Guthry shrugged. "You'll get there."

"Ain't in the cards. Something to what pa kept yammering about the Almighty calling the shots and —"

"Shut up, damn you!" Guthry yelled, suddenly filled to overflowing with such talk. "Heard enough of this Almighty business. There's a God somewhere, I reckon, but not the kind your pa jabbered about —"

"Pa was a God fearing man. He ought've known what —"

"All he knew was what he wanted himself to believe. That Almighty he kept spouting about he made up to suit his own purpose — one that would let him think everything and anything he did was right — killing and all."

"He was plain loco — crazy, all because he thought he was to blame for you, and he got it in his head that the Almighty had given him orders to make up for it by killing you — and anybody that got in his way. Well, I'll tell you something — that's not the Almighty decent people listen to, and for my part I've got a belly full of hearing about it! Now, we've got a long, roundabout ride ahead of us to Lawsonville and I'm warning you — keep your mouth shut!"

"I'll be saying what I please," Rich said coldly. "Ain't no tin-horn badge toter going to tell —"

Savage, ungovernable fury surged through Dan Guthry. He lunged forward, caught the outlaw by the

180

throat, slammed him hard against the side of the coach. For several long moments he hung there, fingers locked upon the man's windpipe gradually closing as the urge to kill Sul Rich, to square up all things in the past drove him with overpowering force . . . And then reason returned. Breathing heavily, blinded by sweat, he settled back on the seat of the swaying coach.

"You're not worth killing — and don't deserve dying," Guthry said in a low voice. "Fact is I'd cooked up a little personal revenge of my own for that stunt you pulled on me back in that coulee near Lawsonville — but I'm forgetting that. You're below even what I had in mind. All I can say is this — for the first time in my life I'm going to enjoy a hanging."

Anger vented, Dan Guthry fell silent, but his eyes never moved from the now silent outlaw. After a time he dug into his pocket for the key to the cuffs encircling Rich's wrists. Releasing one, he looped the chain around one of the door posts and replaced it, thus securing the outlaw to the coach itself and making escape an impossibility. Then opening the opposite door, he climbed out, and clinging to the side of the rocking vehicle, hailed the driver.

"Only want to go far as the next station — one where I can get a stage north."

The bearded old man nodded, looked down at Dan. "That'll be Winesap — a couple of hours' ride from here. What's this all about, Marshal?"

"Not a marshal," Dan said. "He got killed back up the line a ways. I'm a sheriff. Got an escaped killer on my hands. Taking him back to get hung."

"You sure come off that hill in a devil of a hurry —"

"Was two men snapping at my heels. Figured to take my prisoner, hold a party of their own . . . Like for you to explain that to your passengers, tell them I'm begging their pardon."

"Won't hurt them none. Only a couple of drummers. Next stage'll pick them up. Whereabouts you taking your prisoner?"

"Town name of Lawsonville — New Mexico."

The driver leaned far over to the opposite side of the seat, spat a stream of brown juice at the weed clumps rushing by. Inside the coach Sul Rich cursed irritably. The driver grinned.

"Long ride you got ahead," he commented.

"You're sure right," Dan said, climbing back into the vehicle . . . It had been a long ride from the beginning.

CHAPTER
TWENTY-TWO

"Why don't you drag out the brass band, string red, white and blue bunting along the street?" Doc Borden demanded testily. "Might as well make a confounded carnival out of it!"

Mayor Henry Lawson, sitting across the table from the round faced little physician in the hotel's dining room, looked puzzled. "Figured we owed it to him, all he's been through . . . A big welcome — the whole town turned out —"

"Just the point — all he's been through. You send him to hell after one killer, saddle him with another —"

"Now, hold on! Was no way for me to know that Erland Flood wasn't the real Erland Flood. His credentials —"

"Figure of speech, Henry . . . Fact remains that he did have a killer riding with him, and the way that telegram sounded, he barely got through with a whole skin . . . So, he's not going to be in any mood — or condition — to put up with a lot of people crowding around, slapping him on the back and getting in the way."

"He'll be thinking about one thing — locking Sul Rich in a cell and getting him off his hands. Then he can take a deep breath. Takes no imagination to realize that killer will have been like an albatross around his neck from the minute he grabbed him . . . Take my advice, Henry, hold your celebration until after it's all over with — I mean the hanging and everything — then let him know how the town feels about him."

"Maybe you're right, Doc . . . And something could go wrong — Rich get away —"

"Doubt that. What it amounts to is that Dan Guthry bet his life, his self-respect and his reputation as a lawman on tracking down that killer and bringing him back to hang. A lot of pride mixed in there, too. Don't think there'll ever be another prisoner who'll get away from him."

Lawson toyed with his empty coffee cup. "Guess you're right," he said again. "We can wait until after the hanging, then hold the celebration."

"Makes more sense, and it'll be the way Guthry'd prefer it . . . Heard any more from the Governor?"

"Only the reply I got after telegraphing him that the sheriff was getting in today with his prisoner. All he said was let him know when Rich was dead."

"Man of few words," Borden commented dryly, rose, and nodded smilingly to Cathren Keel seated two tables over having her noon day meal, turned for the door. Pausing, he glanced back to Lawson, said: "Pay the check, Mr. Mayor. You're about the only man around here who's got any cash."

Cathren Keel stood at the window of her second floor room in the hotel and looked down on Lawsonville's

184

deserted street. *Getting in today*, Henry Lawson had said; that meant she had a little less than two hours to kill before Dan Guthry and his prisoner arrived. Sighing, she moved back, sat down on the edge of the bed.

Two hours . . . Two weeks . . . Two months . . . It didn't matter. Time had been of little import to her since Lori's death, in reality being no more than an alternation of day and night, a passage of seasons — warm weather, cold weather, the pleasant, the unpleasant, none of it changing or having effect upon that which lay within her.

But killing Jim Rich would.

Such would change everything, but most of all it would salve the terrible, festering hate she held for Rich and for what he'd done to Lori, and fulfill the silent vow she'd sworn as her sister's casket had been lowered into the grave.

Lori . . . She had been so young, so fresh, so filled with hope. Wanted to be a nurse, she'd said over and over, and she had a natural bent for it — always doctoring up injured dogs and cats, fussing and worrying over a little bird she'd found somewhere. With her talent she probably could have gone even further, become a physician, only lady doctors weren't particularly welcome anywhere.

She had planned to send Lori off to a nursing school in St. Louis when she turned eighteen and was sure it was what she really wanted. The dress shop had done well and there'd be no financial strain. They'd talked about it a lot and it was pretty well settled.

185

And then Rich had come along. Jim he called himself then. How Lori met him she never learned, but she hadn't liked him from the start. But Lori saw something in him, a loneliness, perhaps — a rejection, since he seemed to have no friends, and that stirred a pity within her, and she had taken him to her heart as she did the suffering animals she encountered.

One week later Lori was dead — and Jim Rich had vanished. Cathren trembled even yet when she recalled those moments of nightmare. She had come home that evening after closing the shop to find the girl lying across the bed, battered, bruised, semiconscious.

Cathren could guess what had happened in the small cottage at the edge of town where they lived, and had set to work frantically, striving to revive her sister from the abysmal state of shock into which she had plunged. She succeeded only partly, saw moments during which Lori had cried out Jim Rich's name, pleading, begging, but it had ended there, and then, thoroughly frightened, she had gone for the doctor.

When they returned Lori was dead. She had taken the ugly, blunt little derringer pistol they always kept in the chiffonier drawer to ward off prowlers, fired a bullet into her brain.

Cathren had buried Lori in Wichita's cemetery, sold her shop and set out to find Jim Rich. Men sought vengeance when wronged by another, was not a woman entitled to the same privilege?

Dodge City . . . Abilene . . . Denver — she saw them all, and a score more, several times only a step behind Rich, it seemed. And then one day, pausing in a village in northern New Mexico, she learned of a man being held for murder at a town called Lawsonville. Sul Rich they said his name was, but when she found that one of his victims had been a young girl, she knew the search was over.

Catching the very next stage south, she made the short trip, and employing the pretext of looking for a place to settle and open a dress shop, made herself acceptable without arousing suspicion . . . She had her first glimpse of Jim — now Sul — Rich a few days before his trial began, but there had been no opportunity to use the derringer . . . And then, a short time later he escaped.

Now he was coming back — and she would not again fail . . . It would be simple to slip inside the empty jail, wait. When Rich, escorted by the sheriff, stepped into the doorway, she would pull the trigger of the derringer not once but twice, send two bullets tearing into his body, thus make certain he would die.

Afterwards they could do with her what they pleased. She would have finished what she had set out to do, and her mind would be at ease finally — something that could only come to pass when Jim Rich was dead. Let Lawsonville and Sheriff Dan Guthry hang her if they wished; it didn't matter.

She'd never had a life of her own, anyway. Always there had been someone else to think about, look out after. First it had been her mother and Lori; then it had been only Lori — but never herself. You would think that somewhere along the way there would have been something for herself, but there'd been no time . . .

187

And now it was too late. It would have been wonderful, though, to have known love, to have had a man — like Dan Guthry, for example . . .

Dan Guthry . . .

Cathren felt a twinge of regret. In the few days she'd known him he had come to mean more than just a friend accumulated by necessity as she moved on intent in purpose. There had been more to him than the others, it had seemed — and with the intuition of a woman, she knew he was taking better than a passing interest in her.

Dan Guthry was a proud man, and a conscientious one; as Borden had implied in the cafe when she had been frankly eavesdropping, the recapture of his prisoner meant much to him. Now she was going to destroy for him all that he had regained — destroy, too, that mutual feeling, however small, that had sprung up between them . . . And he would have no understanding of either.

Cathren shook her head helplessly, pressed her slim fingers together so tightly the knuckles showed white. This was the hardest part of all, she realized suddenly — hurting Dan Guthry; and for the first time in her life she was conscious of the thrust of personal pain. She was denying herself once more. It was the old story all over again; nothing for her, all for someone else.

Disturbed, she rose, walked to the closet where her suitcase, containing a few odds and ends, lay on the shelf. Taking it down, she rested it on a chair, opened it, and rummaging about, produced the derringer.

188

Replacing the bag, she examined the weapon, making certain both chambers were loaded.

Satisfied, she thrust it into the pocket of the suit she was wearing, recalling in that moment that this was the same outfit she'd had on the day she stood on the hotel porch and waved farewell to Dan Guthry when he rode out with that man who'd claimed to be a U.S. marshal.

She reached then for the small gold watch pinned to her bodice, pressed the knob that released the cover and consulted the black Roman numerals on its face. One fifteen . . . The stagecoach would arrive at two o'clock, or near that. She'd delay another thirty minutes and then go down to the jail. When she was sure no one was watching, she'd slip inside — and be waiting.

The trip from Winesap to Lawsonville had consumed four days and an equal number of coach changes. En-route, through the kindness of fellow lawmen, Dan Guthry had managed to clean up to some extent, procure a weapon, and with the authority issued in a telegram from Mayor Henry Lawson, obtain food and fare for his prisoner and himself.

But now the long, tiring journey was over, and when he looked through the window of the coach as it swung into Lawsonville's empty street and rolled on to the stage depot, a feeling of relief coursed through him. There was no crowd, only Lawson and Doc Borden waiting, and that, too, pleased him. The quicker he got Sul Rich locked in a cell, the better he would like it.

The coach came to a stop. The door jerked open at once and Henry Lawson said: "Good to see you again, Sheriff." Beyond him Borden stood grinning.

"Good to be back," Guthry answered, stepping out.

Reaching in, he caught Sul Rich by the arm, pulled him from the coach. The outlaw was sullen, morose; there was no smirking defiance in his manner now. It was as if he knew he'd never be free again of the man who'd clung so grimly to him — not until the trap dropped from under his feet on the gallows and death claimed him.

"Could use a drink," Guthry said. "Soon as I get my prisoner locked in —"

A shout had gone up along the street. Borden said in a hurried voice: "Better do that quick. They've spotted you."

Dan Guthry nodded, took a firm grip on the chain connecting the cuffs on the outlaw's arms, and circling the rear of the stagecoach, started across the dusty roadway for the jail. He halted abruptly. Two familiar figures, bearded, sweat stained and trail worn, had stepped from the passageway next to the building . . . Lot Maxwell and Juan Severo. The surprise within the lawman changed swiftly to sharp tension.

Lot was holding the old Springfield he'd taken from the Apache that night. Severo had provided himself with an ancient, ornate Mexican pistol. It wasn't hard to figure what had happened; they had doubled back after losing him at the stage stop, crossed the terrible expanse of the Espantoso again, and reached Lawsonville well ahead of him and Sul Rich.

"Who —" Henry Lawson began, but hushed as Guthry shook his head warningly.

"Keep back," the lawman said. "And keep that crowd from coming up." He took a half step in front of Rich, faced Maxwell.

"Give it up, Lot," he called.

The two men only stared, remained poised as if ready to spring into action at the slightest touch. Somewhere in the houses behind the buildings a child was crying, and then from the corner of his eye Dan saw movement within the doorway of the jail — a stir of color . . . Blue. Cathren Keel! She was waiting to welcome him . . . The tension seemed to increase, the hush deepen.

"You hear me, Lot? It's all over —"

"No!" Maxwell yelled, and fired from the hip.

Guthry lunged, took the bullet meant for Sul Rich in his own arm. But the heavy slug was wide of target, only carved a shallow furrow in his flesh. Hanging tight to the outlaw's chain, he drew his weapon.

Crouched, he triggered a shot into the dust at Maxwell's feet. Lot, frantically trying to reload the Springfield, paused. A step away from him Juan Severo also froze, stalled by the deadly promise of Guthry's leveled pistol.

"Don't try it, Lot," Dan warned. "I'll drop you in your tracks. Don't want to — but I will . . . Same goes for you, *viejo*."

Maxwell hesitated. He looked at Guthry for a long breath. His shoulders sagged. Cursing, he tossed the rifle into the street. Dan shifted his eyes to Severo.

"Juan, do you want death?" he asked in Spanish.

The Mexican shrugged, dropped his weapon. Borden said something and then Henry Lawson's voice cut through it: "Somebody pick up those guns! Couple of you grab those men for the sheriff."

Jerking at Rich's chain, Guthry started again for the jail. He heard footsteps behind him. Borden's, he thought, and shook his head.

"Wait'll I'm done with him," he said.

The footsteps ceased. The entrance to the jail was just ahead. Releasing his grip on the outlaw's chain, Dan stepped in behind the man, shoved him roughly.

"Don't stop 'til you're inside."

Rich stumbled slightly, hastily recovered. Beyond him Guthry could see into the room. It was Cathren, waiting just as he had hoped . . . But she was not looking at him. Her eyes, hating, were on the outlaw. In her hand was a heavy caliber derringer pistol.

Sul Rich halted abruptly when he saw her, threw up an arm as if to ward off the bullet. Guthry took a long step, moving to get in between, but suddenly she pulled back, let the weapon fall to the floor, turned to him.

"I — I can't do it, Dan . . . Because of you — after all these years I can't do it."

Guthry pushed Rich through the opening into the cell. Face bleak, he stared at her. "You — why would you want to kill him?"

"My sister Lori — for her," she said. "It's a long, long story — one I'll tell you all about later." She then turned and faced him, this time smiling. "For now, welcome home, Dan Guthry."

192

ISIS publish a wide range of books in large print, from fiction to biography. Any suggestions for books you would like to see in large print or audio are always welcome. Please send to the Editorial Department at:

ISIS Publishing Limited
7 Centremead
Osney Mead
Oxford OX2 0ES

A full list of titles is available free of charge from:

Ulverscroft Large Print Books Limited

(UK)
The Green
Bradgate Road, Anstey
Leicester LE7 7FU
Tel: (0116) 236 4325

(Australia)
P.O. Box 314
St Leonards
NSW 1590
Tel: (02) 9436 2622

(USA)
P.O. Box 1230
West Seneca
N.Y. 14224-1230
Tel: (716) 674 4270

(Canada)
P.O. Box 80038
Burlington
Ontario L7L 6B1
Tel: (905) 637 8734

(New Zealand)
P.O. Box 456
Feilding
Tel: (06) 323 6828

Details of **ISIS** complete and unabridged audio books are also available from these offices. Alternatively, contact your local library for details of their collection of **ISIS** large print and unabridged audio books.